P9-DYB-619

THE MORAL LIFE OF SOLDIERS

BOOKS BY JEROME GOLD

FICTION
The Moral Life of Soldiers
Sergeant Dickinson (originally titled *The Negligence of Death*)
Prisoners
The Prisoner's Son
The Inquisitor
Of Great Spaces (with Les Galloway)

POETRY
Stillness

NONFICTION
The Burg and Other Seattle Scenes (Mostly True Stories)
Paranoia & Heartbreak: Fifteen Years in a Juvenile Facility
How I Learned That I Could Push the Button
Obscure in the Shade of the Giants: Publishing Lives, Volume II
*Publishing Lives Volume I: Interviews with Independent
    Book Publishers*
Hurricanes (editor)

THE MORAL LIFE OF SOLDIERS

Jerome Gold

Black Heron Press
Post Office Box 13396
Mill Creek, Washington 98082
www.blackheronpress.com

Copyright © 1987, 2005, 2013 by Jerome Gold. All rights reserved. All of the characters in this book are fictitious. Any resemblance to persons living or dead is purely coincidental. No part of this book may be reproduced in any manner without written permission from the publisher except in the case of brief quotations embodied in critical articles and reviews.

The stories, "Dead Horses," "John," "Concealments," and "Paul and Sara, Their Childhood," were first published in the collection *Of Great Spaces* by Les Galloway and Jerome Gold. Parts of "Paul's Father" were published in that collection, in the collection *Prisoners* by Jerome Gold, and in *Moon City Review*. A small part of "The Moral Life of Soldiers" also appeared in *Prisoners*.

The author would like to thank Gonzalo Munevar, Susan Munevar and Deanna Spurlock for their critiques of "The Moral Life of Soldiers." The author is indebted to the late Les Galloway for his perceptive comments on several of the stories collected in the first part of this book, "In Georgia."

ISBN 978-1-936364-01-5

Cover art and design by Bryan Sears.

Black Heron Press
Post Office Box 13396
Mill Creek, Washington 98082
www.blackheronpress.com

For Jeanne

CONTENTS

PART ONE

In Georgia

PAUL'S FATHER

I. Paul's Father at the Beginning of the War

On the morning Japan bombed Pearl Harbor, Paul's father was racing Adolphe Menjou, the actor, across the Arizona desert to California. Adolphe Menjou was driving a yellow roadster, Paul's father a forest green convertible. Both men were having the time of their lives.

Six months later, driving east across Texas, Paul's father was chased by a tornado following Route 66. Outside a town a Mexican woman with thirteen kids, or maybe twelve, ran out onto the highway, forcing Paul's father to veer wildly to avoid driving into her or her children. Paul's father did not stop. The tornado blackened the town on either side of the road behind him and then it took the woman and her children.

When Paul's father told the story of the woman and her children—when Paul was thirteen or fourteen and beginning to pull away from his father—he did not emphasize but left implicit their differentness from him, from him and Paul. And anyway, if he had stopped, he could not have saved her and her children, not all of them. And who would decide who would not fit in the car? Anyway, there was no time, not even to stop for one—one child, or the woman alone, perhaps. What did Paul expect from him? Should he have died with them to show solidarity?

Many years after the episode in Texas, driving east again, but through New Mexico, Paul's father was once more pursued by a tornado. In the car with him were Paul's mother, his sister, and Paul. This time, the tornado gaining on them but still a mile or two behind, he stopped and turned the car and drove back west into the twister as fast as he could get the car to go. It was a 1946 Lincoln Cosmopolitan and it weighed more than two tons. It had a V12 engine and it went unswervingly, if with some hesitation, directly into and through the storm. Afterward sand was pitted into the fenders of the car an eighth of an inch and the windshield had to be replaced.

When Paul's father told this story to Paul's uncles and their wives, he did not say that other cars with smaller engines had not turned, but had outrun the twister. Paul and his family met some of their passengers at a café when Paul's father's new windshield was being placed. Paul's father risked the lives of his wife, his daughter, his son, himself. For what?

When he was older, Paul understood that his father had loved speed, hated moral quandaries. And, given the chance to survive, he had loved the violence of embracing his enemy whom he loved more than Paul's mother, his sister, Paul. Though, to be accurate, when he and Adolphe Menjou heard on their respective radios the news about Pearl Harbor, both men slowed their cars.

II. Paul's Father and Paul's Uncle Bernie

When Paul was a boy, he used to go out to the desert with his father and his uncle Bernie, ostensibly to shoot rabbits. Once they followed a mountain lion's tracks until Bernie said, "What are we going to do if we find it?" They were carrying .22-caliber rifles and, from its tracks, they knew it was a big cat.

Once Paul shot a bird at what he thought was a far distance. It turned out to be a hummingbird. Suddenly, seeing it so small and dead, knowing that he had done it, his heart felt as though it were breaking apart. His father said, "Don't you feel bad?" Paul could not say anything. He thought he would cry if he tried to speak.

The best parts about being out with Bernie and his father were driving east through the San Bernadino mountains in the morning, into the sun and what they knew would be a scorching day, and listening to the car radio—the Bob and Ray Show, which made Paul laugh—and then later, after they had walked for a couple of hours, building a small fire so they could have coffee or, in Paul's case, chocolate, and telling stories of their lives. Paul did not tell stories, of course, because he hadn't lived long yet and both his father and Bernie had passed through what Paul was experiencing in his life. Also, Paul did not wish to confide the private parts of his life to them.

Bernie would talk to Paul's father about Elaine, his wife, whom he continued to find desirable, and his son who could piss a stream five or six feet long. When Paul looked at him in disbelief, Bernie said, "Little boys can do that. You lose it as you get older, even at your age." Paul was twelve.

Bernie would talk, too, about his experiences in the navy. He had been in the Battle of the Coral Sea in World War II. He told Paul once that when he was in Hong Kong after the war, another sailor, a larger man, had threatened him. Paul did not know if he had threatened to kill Bernie or to beat him up, but Bernie had been scared. But then he had gotten tired of being scared and had fought the man, using a chair leg to beat him until he could not get up. Afterward, the man left him alone; he was afraid of Bernie now.

Paul's father had not been in the war, at least not as a combatant. He had been on the Manhattan Project at the University of Chicago. Since adolescence, he had been responsible for supporting his mother and sister; his mother did not speak English and his sister spent most of her life in mental institutions. He had had scholarship offers from several universities, including MIT and Stanford, but had had to turn them down in order to work. He went to night school for several years, but never earned a degree.

During the war, the navy had offered to commission him and send him to college to study electrical engineering, but the government would not release him. So he missed out not only on a first-rate education, but also on that indefinable thing that binds men to one another after they have suffered hardship together.

Out in the desert, Paul's father told a story about something that happened after the war. He had been working at Argonne National Laboratories on the edge of the Argonne Forest outside of Chicago. One of the things his particular laboratory did was to separate usable uranium from its ore. Part of the process they employed involved baking the ore in a lead-lined oven.

One day Senator Joseph McCarthy came to inspect the laboratory. Senator McCarthy's star was rising then and he was looking for treasonous persons and acts of perfidy by which to boost it further. During his inspection, Senator McCarthy noted that the uranium ore weighed less when it came out of the baking oven than it did when it was placed inside. The laboratory manager explained that the loss of weight was owing to a chemical reaction between the ore and the lining of the oven.

Senator McCarthy was not to be deceived. He wondered aloud who in the laboratory might be selling the missing uranium to the Russians. He said he would return to re-inspect.

When Senator McCarthy returned, he noted that the uranium ore weighed more coming out of the oven than when it was placed inside. The engineers knew that this was due to the chemical reaction between the ore and the new brick lining of the oven. But they said nothing and waited for the senator's reaction. Their anxiety was needless, for Senator McCarthy was content.

Around this time, someone in Paul's father's laboratory began to wonder what was being done with the radioactive waste the laboratory was producing. Someone asked the engineers and finally one of them admitted that he had been filling Mason jars with it, then burying the jars in the forest. He had not mapped the places where he had buried the jars.

When Paul's father finished telling this story, Bernie laughed about Senator McCarthy and said how typically governmental Senator McCarthy's last response was and how it reminded him of the navy. Then he asked how dangerous was the radioactive waste in the Mason jars.

Paul's father shrugged. He said that not only didn't any-one know where they were buried, but nobody knew how many there were; the man who had buried them hadn't counted them.

III. Paul's Father and the Sailor

Once, a friend of Paul's mother brought her new boyfriend to Paul's parents' house. This was during the war in Korea, when Paul's family lived in Georgia. The boyfriend was in a swabbie's uniform and he made a remark about men who had not served in the military in the last war, even though he himself was obviously too young to have been in. Paul's father smiled and put out his hand as though to shake the younger man's. The sailor extended his own hand and suddenly he was upside down against the far wall of the living room and then he fell off it onto the sofa and rolled off the sofa onto the floor.

"Oh, Herb," Paul's mother said.

Paul's father was smiling genuinely now and offered his hand again, this time to help the other man up. The other man raised his hand, then withdrew it.

"It's all right," Paul's father said. "I made my point."

The sailor put out his hand and Paul's father helped him to his feet. Facing each other, each smiled, Paul's father in friendship, the sailor as though not knowing what to think. The two women laughed from nervous relief. Paul and his sister stared in awe at their father.

They had never seen him do anything like this before. He

was not an especially physical man, as they knew him. He did not go in for violent sports, he did not hunt or fish as some of his friends did. Four years later, when he and Bernie and Paul went out into the desert after rabbits, Paul's father did not shoot; he did not even carry a rifle.

So the sailor got to his feet and he and Paul's father stared at each other, each wearing a kind of smile, and the women laughed and then there was talk and movement and noise as everybody went into the dining room for supper.

IV. What Paul's Parents Did in Georgia (I)

Paul's parents had grown up in Chicago and Paul and his sister were born there, but they all moved to Georgia because his sister was ill and her doctors said she would not live to be ten unless their parents took her to live in a warmer climate. Paul's father found work at the Lockheed plant in Marietta.

After two or three years, Paul's father decided that he wanted to be his own boss and he and Paul's mother thought they could make a success of a restaurant. They opened it in a new shopping center. Its patrons, at least at first, were the workmen who were still building the shops and stores that would compose the center.

Restaurant work was harder than Paul's parents had anticipated, and unrelenting. Paul's father took a leave of absence from Lockheed. Paul's mother worked a regular shift as a cook and also supervised the staff when Paul's father was busy elsewhere. Paul bussed and washed dishes. He worked nine hours a day in the summer and on weekends and holiday breaks from school, and his parents worked longer. His father, a small man, lost forty pounds in his first six months as a restaurant owner.

One evening after closing, seven or eight months after the restaurant opened, Paul sat with his mother, his father, and one of the waitresses at a table. They were taking a break from cleaning up. It was the night they buffed and waxed the floor and Paul had been operating the buffer. The adults were talking about inconsequential things and Paul was listening. Finally somebody decided that they needed to get back to work and they all stood up. Except Paul's mother. She could not get up. Her body would not obey her mind. She started crying, and either Paul's father or the waitress sent Paul on an errand to the kitchen. But Paul did not go. He stayed and watched, and in a moment the weakness passed and his mother stopped crying and pushed away from the table and stood up.

Paul's mother got away from cooking by hiring a man named Curtis Baron. He was a good cook and Paul's parents appreciated his ability. In turn, Curtis appreciated their giving him a job because he was not long out of the state prison in Alabama and not everybody was willing to hire an ex-convict. Curtis was personable as well as a good cook, and he was careful not to offend anyone.

Eventually, after he became comfortable with Paul's parents, he boasted to them that he had more of their silverware at home than they had in their restaurant. They told him to bring it in and he did, in an old army duffel bag. He was right: he had more than Paul's parents had.

They fired him and Paul's mother took over the cooking responsibilities again. But they let him hang around the restaurant because they still liked him and he had no other place to go to be with people. Occasionally Paul's parents hired him to fill a shift when Paul's mother was too tired or had something else to do. Each day after he worked a shift, Paul's mother or father would ask Curtis to return the silverware he had taken the day before. (He seemed to steal only when he was working, as though he saw it as part of his job.) Usually he did, but sometimes he did not, swearing on the latter occasions that he had not stolen any this time, he did not know why.

Finally he left. He told Paul that he was going to leave, that he thought the police were after him, that they believed he had done some burglaries, and the next day he did not come in to the restaurant.

After a few days Paul's parents began to wonder where Curtis was, they had not seen him in a while, and a few days later Paul told them that Curtis had said he was going to go down to Florida. Paul had waited to tell them because he did not know what they might already know, nor what they might do with their knowledge, and he wanted Curtis to get away. Paul's father counted the silverware but could not tell if any was missing.

V. The Last Best Day

They have just come out of the movie house and now Paul's parents and his sister have gone into the supermarket, leaving him to stand at the far edge of the parking lot overlooking the remains of a mixed forest—loblolly pines and hickories and cow oaks—and then, farther, the four-lane highway, and beyond that a lowland swamp.

He is standing at the verge of a shopping center newly built on a high hill they have sliced the top off of to make a level place for commerce and traffic. The sky is pale blue and small white clouds drift across it and he is ten years old and he is wearing a blue and green checked windbreaker, his favorite jacket, against the chill fall day and he has just come out of a movie and he is standing on what is the top of the remains of a hill beside the family car and he's nearly on a level with the small clouds, looking down past the trees onto the plain and the swamp beyond, and he knows exactly where he is and where he belongs and he is ten and he is wearing his favorite jacket and it is the last best day in the history of the world.

VI. The First Dead Man Paul Ever Saw

Paul saw his first dead man one day when he was walking home from school. It was late winter, the beginning of spring. Leaves were green, but sparse. The road he followed took him along the flank of a hill.

At the bottom, the dead man lay. Two men were walking away from him, starting up toward the road. Paul was certain the man was dead, though he could not have said how he knew. Maybe because the man looked so flat, as though constructed in two dimensions. His raised knee fell to the side. It was his left knee. Paul saw everything clearly.

It was autumn, actually, and the leaves were sparse and brown.

The two men were climbing the hill, looking at their feet. Paul saw them. He continued walking, looking back once.

The men had reached the road and were walking in the direction opposite the one Paul was walking in.

At home, Paul turned the television on and off. He poured milk into the sink, emptied the dog's dish into the garbage bag. When his parents arrived, Paul told them what he had seen.

They called the Sheriff's Office and a deputy came over. Paul told him what he had seen.

Don't tell anybody else, the deputy said. Then he went away.

Yes, he told Paul's parents when he came back, the man is where your son said he was and he is dead.

Then the deputy said, It's very important that your son not say anything more. Nor should you.

They didn't, Paul and his parents. Not even to each other. Paul didn't.

He saw a dead man and the men who killed him. He never learned who the dead man was, nor who they were, nor why they killed him.

VII. What Paul's Parents Did in Georgia (II)

The restaurant became profitable at the end of its first year, an accomplishment of which Paul's parents were proud, not having expected to earn money from it until after its second year.

They bought another restaurant, this one with an established customer base, on Highway 41, across from Dobbins Air Force Base. There was a motel beside it and airmen would bring their women friends to the restaurant for a steak and then rent a room at the motel. Unlike the place Paul's parents had in the shopping center, which closed every evening after the early supper trade left, the one on the highway stayed open until midnight, its trade not only the Dobbins airmen but travelers on their way south to Miami or north to Chicago.

· The patrons for the first had changed from workmen to the employees of the other stores in the center and, on weekends, the homeowners who had bought into the tracts that had recently been built in the area south of the town. The latter were settled people, or wanted to be, with young children and dreams of a safe, corporate future. The men worked for the telephone company or were air force officers or senior NCOs or worked for one or another of the manufacturing companies that were coming down from the North in search of cheap labor.

But those who came into the restaurant on the highway were not settled, though they may have been once, or may have wanted to be. Paul met a cowboy from Florida who was on his way to Arizona following a dry summer and a series of fires that had burned enough grazing land in north Florida to put him out of work. He had lived in Florida his entire life and was worried about tearing up his roots. Until Paul met him, he had not known there were cowboys in Florida.

In middle age, sitting at a table by the window in a house in a Samoan village, absorbed in the feel on his skin of the breeze coming through the window, allowing his thoughts to find their own subject, Paul would remember a man sitting at the counter over the remains of his breakfast in the restaurant on Highway 41, reading a newspaper article about the murder of a little girl in Atlanta. Paul's mother poured him another cup of coffee as a waitress swept away his plate and silverware. Paul's mother said how terrible it was about that girl and the man shrugged and said it didn't bother him.

"How can you say that?" Paul's mother demanded.

He shrugged again. "It doesn't bother me. I didn't know her. I don't know her family."

"She was just a little girl. Her family is suffering just like your family would suffer."

The man stood up. "She wasn't part of my family," he said.

"Maybe it will happen to you someday."

The man paid his bill. Paul's mother took his money and gave him his change.

"Maybe," he said.

"Are you going down to Florida?" Paul asked. He was sitting on the counter stool nearest the cash register.

The man smiled at him. "I am."

"You'll be driving through Atlanta."

The man walked outside, still smiling. When Paul turned back from watching him, his mother was staring at him. "You and your mouth," she said, and she let out a series of small, almost silent chuckles.

VIII. The Church and the Dispossessed

Before Paul's father went on leave of absence from Lockheed, Paul's family took in another family that had just moved to the United States from Germany where, it was understood but not talked about, at least in Paul's home, the husband had worked on that country's rocket program during the war. There were the husband, the wife, and a child, a girl

Paul's age. It was not clear to Paul and his sister why the German family had to live with them—his sister had to give up her room and move into Paul's room with him—but they did, although only for a couple of months.

The girl was in the fourth grade with Paul. Later in his life, all Paul could recall of her was that she often farted in class, unable, or perhaps unwilling, to squeeze her farts back. With the first one, she appeared surprised that the other students laughed. After the second or third occasion, her face became inflamed and an embarrassed smile settled on it. This became her expression from then on every time she audibly passed gas.

The teacher explained that farting in class was acceptable in Germany and asked the students to be more tolerant. Some of the students tried and were even successful, but others did not try and looked forward to the next fart so they could laugh again.

After a month or two, the German couple bought a house in a different part of town and they and their daughter moved away. The girl changed schools and Paul did not see her again.

After Paul's parents became restaurant owners, when one of the elders of the Baptist Church approached them about giving a job to someone who needed one, he reminded Paul's father about what he done for the German family. From then on, when the church took in people who were down and out, it often foisted them off on Paul's parents who gave them work and sometimes a place to sleep in their own house, Paul and his sister doubling up again on these occasions.

Once there was a boy and his mother. He wasn't really a boy, but Paul considered him a boy because, although he was twenty-four, he was like a playmate. In the middle of mopping the kitchen floor, he would suddenly ask if Paul wanted to play catch, or he would come over and sit next to Paul at the counter and tell him about a movie he had seen. His mother simply sat through the day, smoking cigarettes at a table in a corner, occasionally scolding her son for his laziness when she saw that Paul's parents were displeased with him. They were likable enough, especially the boy, but when they said thanks and caught the bus to move down to Florida, passed on from one Baptist congregation to another, it was wonderful to see them go.

As soon as the bus pulled away, mother and son waving to Paul's family through the window, they—Paul, his sister, and his parents—broke out laughing. It was spontaneous, and realizing this and seeing one another doubled up or gasping for breath, they laughed all the harder. They laughed until it became too painful to continue, and then they went back to the restaurant on Highway 41 and Paul swept and mopped the floor which had been one of his tasks until the man-boy took it over from him.

IX. Marv and Paul and Davy Crockett

Marv died forty-seven years after he came back from Korea and got married and came South with his bride to spend his honeymoon with Paul's family. He was Paul's favorite uncle. Paul hadn't seen him since his mother's funeral eleven years before, but he flew down to southern California to attend his. At the reception following the service, Paul enjoyed himself, talking with Marv's children, who had suddenly become middle-aged, and other cousins he hadn't seen since they were all small. Then he flew back to Seattle. He was surprised that he didn't feel bad.

A couple of weeks later, as Paul was driving to work, the radio started playing "Christmas in the Trenches," the song—spoken poetry, actually—about English and German soldiers getting up a soccer game in No Man's Land on Christmas Day 1914. Paul started crying; it was several minutes before he was able to stop. The sounds that were coming out of him—even though he was alone in the car, he was embarrassed. It was, of course, his losing Marv that brought on the crying fit. As an adult, Paul hardly saw him, but when Paul was a child, he adored Marv.

It must have been late 1950 or early 1951—it was cold enough that he had to dress heavily for warmth—that he came home from school for lunch one day and found Marv sitting on a wooden chair in the kitchen, talking with Paul's mother. He was in uniform and he looked very sad or very frightened. He and Paul's mother were not joking and laughing as they usually did when they were together, but were talking soberly, just below the range of Paul's hearing. They continued talking as Paul ate, though the subject seemed to have changed. Marv left before Paul finished, hugging Paul's mother after he got into his coat and then walking out the door of the apartment, and Paul's mother began to cry. Paul didn't know what was wrong. If his mother told him, he didn't understand. This must have been just before Marv went to Korea. In middle age, Paul visualized him as he was then: not much taller than Paul's mother, skinny, with a big nose and big ears. A gangly kid. He did not have the presence that came later with size and experience.

Paul and his parents and his sister had moved South from Chicago and were living in Georgia when Marv got out and got married and, not having much money, he and Marian came to stay with Paul's family for their honeymoon. Paul's mother said Marv was sick from malaria and not to expect too much from him.

He and Marian took a Greyhound bus down from Chicago and Paul went with his father to the bus station to pick them up. Paul and his father arrived early. It was a warm day and Paul was thirsty. He found a water fountain but there was a line of people waiting to drink from it. Wandering around, he turned a corner and found another fountain that nobody was drinking from and he went over and got water there. When he was finished, he looked up and saw an old man and woman staring at him. Then the man turned and said to Paul's father who was somewhere behind him, Paul couldn't see where, "Is this your boy?"

"Yeah, why?" Paul heard his father say. Paul had not moved from the fountain. The woman's eyes fixed him to the ground he stood on as if she had planted him there. Paul had never seen such coldness emanate from a person's face. It was entirely expressionless, as though Paul were so alien, not even something living, that there was no point in her trying to communicate with him.

"Your boy is drinking from the colored water fountain."

Paul turned back toward the fountain. When he did this, the woman took a step toward him, then stopped, apparently satisfied that he was not going to drink from it again.

Paul's father walked around from behind the man. "Did you drink from the colored water fountain?"

"No, I drank from that one." Paul pointed to it. He had no idea what his father and the large old man were talking about. When they said "colored water fountain," Paul envisioned water with colors in it. He had not seen any colors in the water he drank.

"That's the colored water fountain. There's a sign."

The old man was right. Affixed to the wall above the spout was a sign, black lettering on a white board, that read "Colored".

"The fountain for whites is over there," the old man said.

"Why did you go to that one?" Paul's father asked.

"Because there was a line at the other one. Nobody was at this one."

The three adults compared fountains. There was no one at the colored fountain; there was still a line at the whites fountain. Everybody in the line was watching the old man and woman and Paul's father and Paul.

"There was a line at this one," Paul's father said. "He didn't want to wait in line." Paul's father was smiling and there was a hint of an attempt to ingratiate in his voice.

"Didn't you see the sign?" the old man asked. His voice had softened.

"No," Paul said. He had already lived in the South long enough to know he was expected to address adult men, especially those he didn't know, as "sir," but this time he did not.

The woman's face softened a little. Paul could see that some people, in other circumstances, might think of her as kindly. He wondered which was the real person.

"He didn't see the sign," Paul's father said.

"You see a sign that says 'Colored' again, you going to drink from that fountain?" the old man said.

"No," Paul said.

"All right," the old man said. He turned to the people in the whites line. Some of them made small smiles. Others' faces remained frozen.

"Come over here, Paul," his father said. "Stay where I can see you."

When Marv and his wife stepped off the bus, Paul could see that his uncle was taller by nearly a foot than he remembered him. And although he was thin, he weighed more than two hundred pounds, Marv told him that evening.

At supper, Paul's father told Paul's mother and his uncle and aunt what happened at the bus station. Later in his life, Paul had a vague sense that Marv said something after listening to Paul's father, but Paul did not remember what it was. Marv had been a soldier in the first racially integrated army in American history. After speaking, Paul's father laughed from shame or rue for the way he had conducted himself, but he had been afraid for his son. What else could he have done? he seemed to be asking. What would have been the consequences of doing what was right?

Paul's mother, or perhaps his Aunt Marian or his uncle asked Paul if he had been afraid. He probably said no. That was how he would have answered, regardless of what he had felt, although in truth he did not remember what he said. He thought he would have denied his own fear out of consideration for his father, as well as to protect his own idea of himself. Of who he was. He was ten years old.

In middle age, Paul did not remember doing much with Marv when he was in Georgia, though he did remember their throwing a baseball back and forth, Marv catching it barehanded, as Paul did not have a glove that fit his hand, and, with Paul's father, they played pop-up. Paul worshipped him. (Paul's father, who did not have a brother, introduced Marv everywhere as "my kid brother-in-law." Paul's father did not like many people, but he liked Marv immensely.) Marv wore his hair in a pompadour and used Brill Cream to work it into the contours he wanted. Paul took up Brill Cream, but he was not able to manage a satisfactory pompadour for about three years, and by that time the ducktail and spit curl were in fashion and he had discovered petroleum jelly.

Later, Paul's sister remembered Marv and Marian buying her and Paul a Monopoly game. Until then, Paul had played chess in the evening with his father and with Marv and Marian, too, or they watched TV. Paul was very aggressive at chess and had screaming nightmares in which the chess pieces came alive and attacked his father, and perhaps Marv and Marian bought the Monopoly set in order to dampen his dreams. Or maybe they bought it so that Paul and his sister would do something together and Paul would leave Marv alone. In retrospect, Paul thought the latter was the true, or truer, explanation.

Only after Marv died did Paul realize how jealous he had been of the time Marv spent with his bride when they were with Paul and his family. He had retained memories of two kinds of emotion he felt during that time: one was adoration for Marv; the other was anger toward Marian when Marv was not paying attention to him. It must have been hard for her. Once, when he tried to butt into a conversation she and Marv were engaged in, she said to Paul, "If he had wanted you to know, he would have told you." Paul was angry enough to say something nasty in return—four and a half decades later, he didn't remember what—that hurt her.

In the early 1950s, Disney ran a TV series on Davy Crockett starring Fess Parker who, because he was so tall and seemed so sure of himself, reminded Paul of Marv. Paul loved that series and insisted that Marv watch it with him. In several of the episodes, Davy Crockett said, "Be sure you're right, then go ahead." Paul later recalled Marv telling him, as they sat side by side on the sofa after Davy spoke, "Remember that." Paul did. The difficulty in following Davy's dictum, of course, was in often not knowing what was right, or in not being able to distinguish what was right from what was self-serving.

At the dinner table, Marv belched. Paul had forgotten about his belches until, at the funeral service, one of Marv's grandchildren talked about them. Paul also had been fascinated by those belches that seemed to go on for minutes without ceasing. Could Marv really breathe and belch at the same time?

Marv began instructing him, until one evening at supper Paul sat back and crossed his arms over his chest, as Marv did his, and tried pathetically to follow Marv's lead. Paul's parents were astounded. His father appeared not to know what to say. (But, silently, he seemed to think it was really funny.) His mother accused Marv of teaching Paul his rude habit. Marv denied it. She turned to Paul and warned him not to imitate Marv.

After supper, when Paul got him alone, he asked Marv to

give him another belching lesson, but Marv declined, saying he didn't want to get Paul's mother angry at him. Once
afterward, Marv belched at the table, catching the attention
of Paul's parents, but apologized immediately, saying it had
just slipped out.

Paul's sister reminded him, not long after Marv died,
that he had had a malaria attack when he and Marian were
staying with them. Paul remembered Marv being sick for a
month, but malaria occurs in forty-eight-hour cycles of fever
and cold and later, when Paul tried to focus his memory, he
doubted that Marv was ill for more than a few days. Paul did
remember Marv being isolated in one of the bedrooms and
then coming out a good deal thinner and quite weak. Paul
remembered asking Marv to do something with him—play
catch?—and Marv telling him he was too tired and then going back into the bedroom.

One afternoon Marv gave Paul his CIB—the Combat
Infantryman's Badge. This is an award that is given only by
the army and only to infantry soldiers who have been in
combat. The CIB is a representation of a flintlock rifle set
against a wreath, both the rifle and the wreath silver or pew-
ter-colored, on a field of light blue. It is fastened to the heart
side of the dress uniform by two pins, positioned above all
other awards and decorations, and sewn above the pocket on
the fatigue uniform, and above the parachute wings, if the
soldier has been awarded them, on the same side. Among
servicemen and –women, it is highly valued, proof that its
wearer has come under enemy fire. Not many soldiers see
combat; most, even in an area where there is fighting, are
support troops. In Korea, in the army, only one of ten or
twelve was a combat soldier.

Paul did not know why Marv gave him his CIB. He did not know what it signified to him, nor what he thought Paul would make of it. Later, Paul did not remember Marv's saying anything when he handed it to him, and he was not even certain that it had happened on the brisk, sunny afternoon that he recalled Marv giving it to him, though he could, in his memory, see Marv's open hand, and see yellow sunlight coming from behind the impression Marv's body made against its background, and feel a chill again, as if it had been brought on a breeze.

In 1966, having returned from Viet Nam and needing someone to talk to, Paul went to see Marv who, a few years before, had moved out to California, following Paul's family. People who have been in war often, afterwards, find themselves searching for what is genuine in other people and have little tolerance for what is not. Paul went to see Marv because he trusted him.

They sat at the kitchen table and Marian brought them coffee. It was late morning and it was sunny on the other side of the window. Sometimes one or another of Marv's and Marian's kids would come into the kitchen with a question or to see what was going on.

Paul and Marv exchanged silly but cynical stories about their respective wars and about the army, which, for the ground soldier, seems never to change, regardless of the vaunted transformations technology purportedly brings. The pattern of the story-telling was that Paul would tell one and then Marv would match it with one from his own experience.

The last one Paul told was about a soldier whose patrol stopped for lunch. After eating, men tossed the cardboard and cans from their C-rations into the fire. Someone threw in an unopened can, which, in a moment, burst from the heat of the fire and shot jelly out in a wad, hitting Paul's friend in the mouth, burning it and splitting his lip. As the lip would not stop bleeding, he was medevac'd out of the field. Eventually he was awarded a purple heart for his wound.

Paul asked Marv about his purple heart. Paul's mother had told him that Marv had gotten it for having fallen into a foxhole and breaking a rib.

What actually happened, Marv said, was that he was trying to evade machine-gun fire and jumped into a foxhole, breaking his rib that way. (At the reception following Marv's funeral, Paul was telling this story to Marv's children when Marian came into the room. She said that he had indeed jumped into a foxhole, but his rib was broken because he came down on another man's—a dead man's—helmet; when Marv looked, he saw that the man's face had been shot away. It was six or seven years after Marv told Paul what he wanted him to know that he told Marian what he wanted her to know.)

Swapping stories, Paul had become unsettled even as he found some of them darkly funny. Finally he was shaking so badly that he could not get the coffee to his mouth without sloshing most of it out of the cup. Marv was having the same problem. Paul had come back from war only weeks before, but Marv had been back for fourteen years. Yet his memories were apparently as vivid as Paul's. Paul did not know then that this kind of memory does not leave you, that it may sleep for a while, for years, even decades, but it is still there, waiting to surface under provocation.

They set their cups down without trying to drink any more. Marian invited Paul to stay for lunch, but he declined.

He and Marv did not talk to each other about their wars again. Neither did they talk about Davy Crockett or baseball or malaria. Later in Paul's life, he would do things that would have appalled Marv, had he known about them. But who knows what is right or wrong until things turn out badly.

X. Sixth Grade

Paul had a teacher for the sixth grade, Mrs. Hawes, who was from New York. Like Paul's father, her husband had gotten a job in the defense industry and Mrs. Hawes had moved to Georgia with him. It was she who told the children in Paul's class that southern schools were to be integrated next year. She explained what that meant. Most of the children did not know that black kids and white kids were prohibited from attending the same school. The kids in Paul's class did not see black kids in their daily lives, so did not think about them. If they were to think of them, they would have assumed that black kids attended a different school because they lived in a different part of town.

The only black person the children in Paul's class saw on a daily basis was Mr. Brown, the school janitor, a reserved, older man who never lost his composure. When Mrs. Hawes told the children in Paul's class why school integration had been ordered and how black people had been treated for so long, some of the girls began to cry. They had had no idea.

After school they found Mr. Brown in the hallway and gathered around him, sobbing. Mr. Brown did not lose his composure. He smiled in sympathy with their tears, careful not to touch any of them. His eyes showed utter bewilderment.

XI. Boy Scouts

Jimmy, Paul's scoutmaster, had been born in Georgia but had lived in the North. He had lived in Chicago and had gone to some of the same nightclubs Paul's parents talked about. He had been a bouncer at the Chez Paree, Paul's father's favorite club, but they had not known each other there. After he was a bouncer at the Chez Paree, Jimmy was in the Air Force. This was during the Korean War. He had taught airmen hand-to-hand combat. He was an expert in judo. Out with his scout troop during overnight camp-outs, he would sometimes wrestle two or three boys at the same time, one arm tied behind his back. He always defeated them. Jimmy was not Paul's uncle Marv; Paul did not worship him, but he almost did.

When Jimmy returned to Georgia after his years away, he worked at a number of jobs that held no meaning for him. This was when he became a scoutmaster. It was in his capacity as Paul's scoutmaster that he met Paul's father. Eventually he asked Paul's father if he would recommend him for a job at Lockheed, and Paul's father did.

Paul's father liked Jimmy and his wife, and occasionally they would come over to Paul's house for dinner. Once, sitting in the living room after supper, the grown-ups talked about what was going to happen next year. Although Jimmy's kids were small, not yet old enough to go to school, he was concerned. Eventually they would go to school and he did not want them to go to school with Negro kids. Paul thought it was interesting that Jimmy never used the words "nigger" or "nigra," but still expressed prejudicial feelings.

Either Paul's mother or his father asked why not and Jimmy said he just didn't. He was all for Negroes being equal to whites, he did not mind that at all, but he did not want their children going to school with his children. Paul's parents tried to get him to tell them why he didn't, but he seemed unable. This was the last time Jimmy and his wife came over to Paul's house, or one of the last times. Things began to move very fast soon afterward and Paul did not see much of him again.

In fact, he saw Jimmy now as a little tarnished. Blemished. After that evening, he separated himself from Jimmy a little. It was not something he intended, but he found himself listening less to what Jimmy said, no longer seeking him out after scout meetings to talk with him. And then Jimmy was gone. The demands of his job, the overtime—he no longer had the time for scouting.

Someone else took Jimmy's place in the troop. Under the new leadership, scouting became more formal. You were penalized if you missed a meeting without an acceptable excuse, and you were penalized if you did not wear your uniform to meetings or if your uniform was not complete or if you did not snap your salute. Scouting had become militarized, though Paul did not know enough then to have expressed it that way. He had liked scouting when it was fun, but he did not like it now. He stopped attending the meetings.

XII. On Highway 41

Once a bus filled with soldiers pulled up in front of the restaurant on Highway 41. As they filed inside, the staff got
busy. Until he walked in, no one noticed that one of the soldiers, the second or third from the end, was black. But then
the cashier saw him and she got Paul's father.

Paul's father came out from the back of the restaurant
and explained to the soldiers that the law prohibited him
from serving black people where white customers ate. He
was apologetic and, seeing his face, Paul believed he was
ashamed of what he was doing. Paul's father said he could
serve the black soldier in the kitchen or he could bring his
order to him on the bus.

The black soldier understood. He appeared to appreciate
Paul's father's dilemma and the humiliation he was suffering.
Paul's father, for his part, seemed on the verge of laughing
hysterically or breaking down into tears.

Several of the white soldiers were angry and did not try to
conceal their anger. They talked of simply going somewhere
else to eat, but then realized that wherever they might go
in the South, they would run into the same situation. They
accused Paul's father and the cashier and a waitress—all the
restaurant help they could see—of racial prejudice, focusing
particularly on Paul's father because they recognized from his
accent that he was from the North. For a moment or two,
Paul thought they might attack his father or try to wreck
the restaurant, and the coppery taste of adrenalin filled his
mouth.

Finally, while some soldiers sat down at the counter or
at tables, others had their orders dished onto paper picnic

plates and they took these into the bus and ate there with the black soldier.

After they ate, as Paul and his father collected the trash from the bus and stuffed it into paper bags, some of the soldiers apologized for the things they had said, while making it clear that they believed they were in the right, and, if not Paul's father personally and the cashier and everyone in the restaurant they had abused, then the South itself was fucked up.

Paul's father apologized again to the black soldier and the soldier said it was all right, he understood.

XIII. How Paul and His Family Came to Georgia and How They Left

1

Paul looked out the window while Mommy fixed supper. The snow was all black in the street where the cars ran over it, but on the sidewalk it was still white. It was squishy in the street but it was still squeaky on the sidewalk. He wanted to go outside but Mommy said it was too cold out and it was getting dark now and anyway supper would be ready soon.

Paul was not hungry but Mommy insisted. We'll eat early before Daddy gets home, said Mommy. We'll play a trick on Daddy. Paul wanted to eat with Daddy but he liked tricks, so he said, All right, but who are you going to eat with? I'll eat a little bit with you and a little bit with Daddy when he gets home, Mommy said. So Paul ate even though he was not hungry and Mommy ate just a little bit.

After a while Daddy came home, looking very tired. He

had to ride forty-five minutes on the El to work and forty-five minutes on the El from work, and the two rides and the crowding and the constant voices in so many different tones and inflections and the jostling and poking in addition to whatever happened at work made him tired.

At work, where he worked on things for the government that he couldn't talk about, people respected him. He was a star, Paul had heard one of the men his father worked with say one evening when the man and his wife were eating supper with Paul's parents. Paul's father was confident that he would rise from where he was in his life. Paul heard his father say that, or something like that, later that night.

When Daddy came home Mommy was very nice to him and told him that dinner was ready and Daddy was hungry and he and Mommy sat down at the table. But then Daddy asked, Why wasn't Paul eating? And because it was a trick, Paul answered, Because I don't want to, that's why. Because it was a trick he made his voice very snotty-like, as if he were bigger than his father.

Daddy got up so fast that Paul could not think, and he could not think either because of the horrible expression on Daddy's face. And Daddy grabbed Paul and picked him up and shook him up and down, up and down, up and down, bouncing Paul's feet on the sofa, and Paul could feel something inside his head shaking around and his teeth were hitting against each other and something inside his stomach was jiggling around too. And Mommy was sitting at the table eating her dinner with her fork very slowly, and Daddy was shouting.

Later Paul heard Mommy telling Daddy that it had all been a trick and Daddy came into Paul's room where Paul was in bed because of his stomach and all the bouncing, and Daddy said he was sorry and Paul could see that Daddy was and said, That's okay, Daddy, you just didn't give me a chance to explain, and Paul felt his throat get choky. He saw that Daddy felt that way too, and in his eyes too. And Daddy said, I know, and they kissed goodnight like they did every night and Daddy went out and everything was all right again.

2

Something was wrong. It was nighttime but the doctor was here. Paul recognized his voice even though he couldn't hear well enough to know what the doctor was saying. He climbed out of bed and went into the front room. The doctor said the word "tonight." When Paul went into the front room he thought his parents would be angry with him for being out of bed so late. He didn't mean to go into the front room, he had meant only to listen at the door, but he hadn't been able to hear very well and then the door opened somehow and he found himself in the room with his mother and father and the doctor.

His mother's and father's faces looked strange. He could not understand what their faces were saying to him. The doctor looked strange too.

"Get your clothes on," his father said. "Get dressed."

"What's wrong?" Paul asked.

"Help him get dressed," his mother said to his father. She was crying, not with her whole face but with only her eyes.

"What's wrong?"

His father was taking him to his aunt's house. His mother had taken his sister and gone with the doctor. His sister was sick. She was going to the hospital. No, she wasn't going to die, his father said. She was just sick and she would have to stay in the hospital for a while. She would have to have an operation. It was nothing serious. Paul would have to stay with his aunt for a while, for a few days, for a week or two. He could go to school with his cousin. He liked his cousin, didn't he? And he liked his aunt?

He liked his aunt but he didn't like the way she smelled. She smelled like old milk, as if somebody had forgotten to drink her and she was still sitting in a glass on the table. She gave him milk and cookies to eat while she talked with his father.

When his father left, she smiled at him. He knew she was trying to make him feel less lonely. But he didn't like her anymore. He poured the rest of his milk in the sink.

His sister was in a big crib with four little tricycle wheels. She looked dopey. She was all doped up, his father said. She didn't know anything. She just looked at him. She had plastic tubes sticking out of her arms and legs.

"Say hello to your sister," his mother told him.

"Hi," Paul said.

His sister just looked at him.

"Hi," Paul said again. "Can she hear me?" he asked his father.

"She probably hears you," the doctor said. The doctor was standing next to his father. This was a new doctor. The old doctor had died. Of a heart attack.

"But she can't say anything," Paul said. He said it as a matter of fact, as something he had observed.

"She'll be able to talk to you tomorrow. She's not feeling very good right now."

The nurse wheeled her away. To her room, his father said.

"Goodbye," Paul said.

Paul and his father and mother drove home. It had been a long time since they had driven home in the car together. Usually it was just Paul and his father. It felt different with his mother in the car now. It felt nice but it felt different.

"What do you think?" his father asked.

"About what?" said his mother.

"About moving."

"Do we have a choice? The doctor said another winter in Chicago would kill her." His mother began to cry.

"How would you like to move to Georgia?" Paul's father asked him.

"I don't want to," Paul said.

"It's warm there all year round. And they have big juicy peaches there. Georgia peaches. Haven't you ever heard of Georgia peaches?"

"I don't want to. I'll never see Mickey and Danny and Jimmy and Bobby again if we go there."

"You'll see them again," his mother said.

"How?" Paul demanded.

"They can visit us in Georgia."

"They won't. I'll never see them again."

"We don't have a choice," his mother said. She was crying again. She had never been out of Chicago except to her parents' cottage on the Fox River. Paul's father had once lived in California.

3

Paul lived with his parents and sister in Georgia in a town called Marietta. His third-grade teacher told the class that Marietta was named for the two daughters, Mary and Etta, of one of the founding fathers of the town, a man whose name was Cobb. Marietta was the seat of Cobb County. Inscribed in the frontal stone of the courthouse was "Reconstructed 1868." The teacher said that before The War Between The States one hundred thousand people lived in Marietta. Marietta had been bigger than Atlanta. But General Sherman burned Marietta on his March To The Sea. Now only twenty thousand people lived in Marietta, and it was smaller than Atlanta.

Paul's fifth-grade teacher said that if the schools were integrated nigras would go to school with white students and would be in the same classrooms. Paul thought that "nigras" meant Negros but he wasn't sure. He couldn't always understand what his teacher said. It had been more than a year before he recognized that "all" could mean "all" or "awl" or "oil." Paul understood what "nigger" meant, and that his parents did not permit him to say that word, but he had never heard anyone say "nigra" until now. He thought maybe his teacher could say "Negro" but didn't want to.

4

Paul's parents owned a restaurant outside of town on Highway 41 and employed as a cook a Negro whose name was Chuck. Chuck was a fine cook, an excellent cook, and Paul's parents and his sister and he liked him personally, but he lived in Tacoa and he didn't own a car. This meant that he had to rely on his friends to drive him to work and to pick him up afterward, so that he was often late going in either direction. Because he had such a talent for cooking, a rare thing in Marietta's restaurant establishments, Paul's father decided to buy him a car, an older car, inexpensive but reliable.

Paul and his father went to a lot in Tacoa where his father picked out a sky-blue Chevy that met his requirements, leaving the car in the lot until he deposited money enough into his account to pay the whole amount by check. Paul's father—a child of the Depression—distrusted credit; he despised the idea of being owned by anyone.

Two days later Chuck called from his home and asked Paul's father to hurry up to Tacoa to pay for the car because those men who owned the car lot were crazy. It was not clear what was going on or how they were crazy.

As he and his father pulled into the lot, Paul noticed a two-by-four plank with two nails sticking out of it at one end. He thought that someone should move it before a car ran over it and punctured a tire. When he got out of the car, he started to go over and pick it up, with the idea of tossing it out of the way of where cars might drive, but his father was already going inside and Paul went after him. He made a mental note to move the board before they left the lot.

The car lot was owned by two brothers. One of them had a very fat, thick neck. The other was smaller, with a throat that made small pimples against the razor's pull. When Paul's father stepped into the office, the larger brother said, "Mr. Donaldson, why didn't you tell us you were buying this car for a nigger?"

Before Paul's father could say anything, or perhaps he did say something, this brother, the big one, the one with the thick, sweating neck and red-meat fists, slammed into him. The other brother, the one with the scrawny, stubbly throat, slid behind Paul's father and either held him back or kept him from falling, Paul couldn't be certain which. It was over very fast. After a minute, or maybe less, the larger brother stepped away and the smaller brother let go of Paul's father's arms and Paul's father rolled across the floor with his knees drawn up. There was quite a lot of noise in Paul's ears and when the big and little brothers turned toward him wearing expressions of startle or surprise on their faces, Paul realized that he had been screaming and swearing hysterically throughout the beating. He became aware, too, that he held in his hands the two-by-four plank with the two nails in it; he didn't remember having run outside to get it, though clearly he must have.

The two brothers were staring at him. The smaller one started toward him and Paul raised the board as though to smash him with it and he moved back.

"Mr. Donaldson, tell your son to put the board down," one of the brothers said.

Paul's father did tell him this, but Paul refused because he did not trust these men not to hit his father again once they could do it without incurring harm to themselves. Finally the two brothers convinced him that they would not hit his father any more and Paul turned and threw the board outside. On the floor was a fair amount of blood and teeth. The bigger brother turned to Paul's father who was on one knee now, and said quietly but loudly, "We don't like you damned Yankees coming down here and telling us how to run our affairs."

Paul and his father drove back to the restaurant to tell
Paul's mother what had happened and that they would be
going to the courthouse to inform the District Attorney of
what had happened and to begin the process that would obtain either justice or revenge. Paul's father pulled into a parking stall, then sent Paul inside alone because he did not want
people to see him looking as he did. It took Paul a while to
convince his mother to come outside. She thought his father
was playing a joke on her, getting her to come outside and
then somehow tricking her, and she was not in a frame of
mind to entertain jokes. She had her own news.

A waitress followed her out, perhaps to defend her against
Paul's father's trick, perhaps not. Perhaps she was the one
Paul's father had slept with; perhaps she was trying to control the flow of information. The waitress understood first
that something bad had happened and she returned to the
doorway to observe from there. Later, when Paul remembered this scene, he was both at the doorway, standing beside her, observing his parents, and also standing beside the
car, watching and listening to them speak.

Paul's mother did not seem to know what to think. First
her face did one thing, then it did another. On it was surprise, then humor, then surprise again—all of this before she
or Paul's father said a word. She did not give her news then.
Later, Paul did not remember her saying anything at this
point. On the other hand, he remembered his father opening the door to get out of the car and his mother insisting
that he not. So maybe she did tell him what happened and
maybe his impulse was to go and look, and maybe she told
him it could wait.

When Paul's father told her he was going to see the District Attorney, she tried to talk him out of it. She wanted him to forget that he had been beaten up. "Just forget about it," she said. Of course he could not. Paul's father wanted justice or revenge. He wanted it all never to have happened, but he was not able to deny that it had.

Homer Holmes was the District Attorney of Cobb County. He had a fine leather office in the courthouse in Marietta. Waiting with his father in the corridor to see Homer Holmes, Paul couldn't keep his eyes from a girl with straw-and-sand hair who was breast-feeding her baby; she was not much older than he was. Many other people were in the corridor and they couldn't take their eyes off of Paul's father.

The District Attorney had a thick, sweaty neck and large meat-and-knuckle hands. He placed Paul's father under "technical arrest" for disturbing the peace of the public by presenting himself openly with such a face. He told Paul's father to go home and to remain there until notified that he could leave. The District Attorney was a cousin by blood to the two brothers in Tacoa whose business it was to sell used cars.

The neighbors from across the street were gentle, slow-speaking people from Alabama. They came to visit, sympathize, advise. The husband shook his head sadly and said, "Herb, you shouldn't have got involved in our affairs." The wife had a dead grandfather who had lost a leg in The War Between The States.

Paul passed his twelfth birthday fishing on the Chattahoochee River. Evenings, he bussed and washed dishes in his parents' restaurant. On occasion he locked himself in the bathroom where he would rehearse jab and cross, finishing with a blood-splattering haymaker. Afterward he would sweat and breathe heavily and deeply and he would run cold water on his wrists to calm himself and take the flush from his face.

He would be six feet six inches tall.

He would be broad but lean and have sledge fists.

He would concentrate steel hatred into lethal shafts directed from his eyes.

5

On a rack beside the cash register postcards were displayed for sale. On one was a cartoon drawing showing an office door with an opaque glass window. Depicted as a shadow on the window was a man sucking a woman's breast. On the doorknob hung a sign that said "Out To Lunch."

Homer Holmes, the District Attorney of Cobb County, determined that Paul's parents were selling pornographic literature and came with the Sheriff to close down the restaurant. While the District Attorney was announcing his intention to Paul's parents, Paul asked the Sheriff if he and the District Attorney were in the Ku Klux Klan. The Sheriff made a small smile. "No," he said.

The people who owned the motel next to the restaurant offered to buy it for a price only a little less than what Paul's parents thought the restaurant was worth. The people who owned the motel were attractive, gracious people who had a daughter whom Paul had liked. She had dark hair, darker than Paul's own, and a blotchless complexion. She had a self-knowing, comforting way of speaking, as though all things, even the saddest things, were inevitable. Paul had liked her very much.

The leader of the Baptist Church in town saw Paul and his father one day on the street and came over to them. Paul was surprised that the Baptist leader did not pretend that he hadn't seen them. "I'm sorry this happened to you, Mr. Donaldson," he said, as though he had been surprised to hear that something had happened, as though things happen to people inexplicably. He was dismayed to hear that Paul's parents had sold their restaurant on Highway 41, but he knew, of course, that they had sold the one in the shopping center, what was it? a year ago now? He smiled at Paul.

Many of Paul's mother's family had moved to California from Chicago. Paul's father used to live there, in California. Now he had a job in the aircraft industry in Los Angeles. Only a month after the people who owned the motel next door made the offer to buy the restaurant Paul, with his parents and sister, began the drive to California.

6

Paul went to school with his cousin. Paul's cousin liked to pick fights with other kids and then run to find Paul. Paul fought almost every day although he was always afraid. His cousin never fought.

On Saturdays Paul went to the movies with his cousin and his sister when she was well enough. One movie was a gangster movie. It starred Richard Conte as a gangster who was betrayed. Richard Conte looked like Paul's father. There were many killings and beatings in the movie and Paul could not watch these scenes when they showed men bleeding. When Richard Conte was killed at the end of the movie, Paul could not watch that scene.

At school a gang of boys surrounded Paul and pushed him around. They told him his mother fucked dogs and blew sailors. They said he didn't know who his father was, and his mother couldn't be sure. They told him they were going to drag him off to the boys' toilet and make him eat shit. There were eight or ten in the gang and other kids stopped to watch. Girls were watching, and one who was Paul's friend was angry with him for allowing himself to be humiliated. When the bell rang the ringleader punched Paul in the stomach and Paul went down. He stayed down while the ringleader and others called back demeaning things as they left for class. The ringleader's name was Willy.

Paul caught Willy in the bathroom and broke Willy's nose. Paul caught Willy again and bloodied his mouth. Paul caught one of Willy's friends and made him drink water out of the toilet. Paul caught another of Willy's friends and hit him with a trash can lid until he couldn't get up. Paul had steel taps put on his shoes. He caught one of Willy's friends and kicked his legs until the kid cried. Paul was always afraid, even when he slept, and when finally Willy moved away to Texas and Paul didn't see either Willy or his friends anymore, he felt wonderfully relieved.

Paul had a friend named George who was very large but very nice. Paul's parents called him "the gentle giant." One day, Paul's father asked him if he thought he could beat up George. Paul wanted to say no, but he said instead, "I don't know." Finally he said, "I think I can."

He would be six feet six inches tall.

He would have sledge fists.

He would concentrate steel hatred in his eyes.

It didn't hurt. He thought it would, but even as he struck himself he knew that at worst he was raising a few lumps, he wasn't punching out his teeth or breaking the bones in his face. It was strange: even through the self-beating he was able to think, to gauge the effect on his father. Yet the rage was real: the redness of it!

After Paul stopped crying he lay exhausted on the bed. His father left him then, and Paul heard his steps leading into the kitchen where his aunt and uncle and cousin were with his mother and sister. "He was hitting himself," Paul heard his father say. Bewilderment was in his voice.

Paul's cousin appeared at the bedroom door. "Can I come in?"

"Yes."

"They're eating now."

"I'm not hungry."

"I'm not either. I ate a whole turkey leg and part of the other one before your sister saw me."

Paul laughed.

"How come you were hitting yourself?"

Paul said nothing.

"You don't look like you hit yourself very hard."

"He didn't even hit them back!"

"What?"

"When they were beating him, he didn't even fight back! He didn't hit them once! He didn't even try!"

"He said he was afraid of what they would do to you."

"He didn't even try!"

"Maybe you should go to sleep now."

Paul hoped that his father had heard him shouting. He hated his father.

Paul's father sat down on the edge of the bed. It was almost dark now. Paul did not remember sleeping.

"When those two gorillas were hitting me, all I could think about was you. Do you remember yelling at them to leave me alone?"

"I remember screaming. I don't remember what I was saying."

"Do you remember what they said?"

"No."

"They told me that if you didn't put the board down they would beat you up too."

"It wasn't my fault!" Paul screamed.

He was crying. It was something he couldn't control. His chest hurt so much it frightened him. "I love you, Daddy," he managed to get out from the constriction of his throat.

"I love you too, Paulie," his father said, holding him.

He would be six feet six.

He would have sledge fists.

"Well, what do you think?" Paul's father asked.

"I don't care what you do," said Paul's mother.

"It would mean more money."

"Do whatever you want."

The corporation Paul's father worked for had offered him

a vice-presidency contingent on his joining a society that stood against Communism, blacks, and Jews, and made clandestine campaign contributions to particular political candidates. All of the corporation's vice-presidents were members of that society, Paul's father said. And Paul's sister was sick. That had to be considered; there were going to be expenses, even with the insurance.

"Do whatever you want," Paul's mother said again.

Paul's father said, "They ought to hang them from lamp poles, teach the bastids a lesson."

"Who?" Paul asked.

"The niggahs!"

Paul lived with his parents and sister in a sprawling frame house in Orange County. There were three bedrooms and a den, a living room, a dining room, a kitchen with all the conveniences, a recreation room, two bathrooms, a four-car garage, a wishing well in the front yard, fruit trees in the back, and three-quarters of an acre of lawn and shrubs surrounding. Paul's father commuted from affluence to work every day. Evenings and weekends, he puttered. Paul's sister was very often ill. His mother watched television.

Paul's father had a heart attack one day while at work. No damage was done to the heart, the doctor said, which was unusual, considering the symptoms, but the symptoms were real enough. Paul's father experienced his second heart attack at the entrance to the corporate campus immediately upon his return to work after recovering from the symptoms of the first. The symptoms of the second killed him.

At his father's funeral a ruddy, thick-waisted man who

had worked with his father told Paul how tragic it was that
Herb in the prime of his life should be killed in a freeway
accident. "It makes no sense," said the red-faced man.

Paul would be six feet six inches tall upon his return.

He would be broad but lean and have sledge fists.

He would concentrate steel hatred into lethal shafts directed from his eyes.

He wouldn't. He couldn't.

He would never go back.

Amplification: Something Else that Happened on the Day of the Beating and What Paul's Mother May Not Have Told His Father

On the day of the beating Paul's father intended to work in
the back room of the restaurant—the banquet room, which
was open to customers only in the evening. Taxes would be
due soon and he and Paul would work on their preparation
together. Paul would go through the receipts and recite the
numbers and his father would punch them into the adding machine. His father could do both tasks without Paul,
of course, and more efficiently—Paul would have questions
about particular receipts and his father would have to stop
his fingers' working in order to answer them: there are different amounts on this one: which did he want? The print on
this one is so light I can't read it—but, as was the case with
lawn work, gardening, and building a fence around their
back yard, he wanted Paul's company.

They had set the adding machine and paper and pencils
and some ledgers on one of the tables when Chuck called.

Something was wrong, he told Paul's father. The men he was buying the car from were crazy and he needed to get over to the lot right away. Paul's father had planned to pick up the car on the following day, but because of the fear in Chuck's voice he decided to go now. Paul went with him. There was no reason why he should not; they were going to spend the day together anyway. And so they went to Tacoa and Paul's father was beaten and ultimately Paul and his father and mother and sister left Georgia. Paul's father never learned—at least he never told Paul—what the men who owned the car lot told Chuck to frighten him so

But he learned something else, possibly when he and Paul returned to the restaurant, or perhaps later. Between the time his father and Paul left for Tacoa and the beating that awaited them, and the time of their return to the restaurant, something happened that Paul's mother wanted to tell his father about when they returned, but may not have. A car had turned off the highway and driven through the brick wall of the banquet room and into the room itself, massing tables, chairs, and all else that was before it against the far wall in a porcupine jumble of planes and spines, table tops and chair seats and the legs from all of them. When one of the cooks went back to turn off the ignition, the rear tires were still milling against the floor tiles. Paul saw these tiles the next day, their surfaces rubbed black, scorched. Paul's father pointed them out to him.

The driver of the car was dead. The police told Paul's parents the next day. He apparently had had a heart attack while at the wheel and died immediately as the car swerved off the road. The police found his body on the floorboards. The cook who turned off the ignition had not noticed it or, if he had, did not say anything about it.

In later years Paul's mother used to say that maybe it was all for the best: if Paul's father and he had stayed to work on the taxes, both of them would have been killed. Paul's father's response was that God could have gotten them out of the banquet room without sending them to Tacoa. Paul himself did not feel grateful to God.

Paul's father seldom referred to the beating he received as what it was—a beating. He alluded to it elliptically, if he alluded to it at all, or simply left the allusion unsaid, knowing that Paul's mother, his sister and Paul understood what he did not want to say.

Addendum

Twenty-one years after Homer Holmes drove Paul's family from Georgia, Paul was working in Seattle as Chief of Security at Providence Hospital. This was shortly before Providence renovated to become the medical center it is now. At the information desk just inside the main entrance sat a woman who volunteered at the hospital two or three times a week. On this day Paul saw sorrow on her face and he asked what was wrong. Her daughter's father-in-law had died this morning during open-heart surgery, she said. Her daughter and her husband would be flying out to Georgia for the funeral. It was terribly sad. He had been an admirable man, and still young.

"Where in Georgia?" Paul asked.

"Marietta. It's a small city near Atlanta. He was the District Attorney there."

"I used to live there."

"Really? How odd that we should be talking today. When did you live there?"

"Oh, a long time ago. I was a little boy."

"Well, perhaps you heard of him. He was the District Attorney for years and years. His name was Homer Holmes."

After a moment Paul said, "I knew him. My family knew part of his."

"Really! And we're talking today, three thousand miles away from where he died, and we both knew him. When did you last see him?"

"I left Marietta over twenty years ago."

"Still, how strange it is that you knew him and that we're here now, talking about him. The world really is very small. Would you mind if I gave my daughter your name and told her about our conversation?"

"I don't mind. But it's my father's name that the Holmes family may remember." Paul told her his father's name. "Or they may not."

Paul called his mother that night and told her that Homer Holmes had died and how he knew. She said, simply, "Good."

Paul's mother died twelve years later. It was then, in the weeks before she died, that she told Paul of his father's infidelity. Paul did not know until she told him that his father had fallen in love with one of the waitresses who worked for them. His mother did not tell Paul when she found out; Paul did not think she knew on the day his father was beaten up, the day she and the waitress who, Paul now suspected, was his father's lover, rushed out of the restaurant to learn what had befallen him. Paul did not know when she found out, but it was soon after he and his family arrived in California that he noticed his parents' estrangement from each other.

In the days before his mother died, more and more of her feeling about his father came out, until Paul thought that she hated him more deeply than she loved him, that by the time he died she may not have loved him at all. She accused Paul, too, of having betrayed her, although she did not say in what way.

Paul's sister is well for now. She has encountered one malady after another and she has fought them off, though not without residual damage. It seems that once one thing in the body goes out of harmony, other things follow.

Life proceeds by indirection.

DEAD HORSES

Bob put the muzzle of the Weatherby an inch from the beetle. The diameter of the muzzle was only a little narrower than the length of the insect. Bob pressed the trigger. The rifle was a .300 magnum and it bucked and made a roar that reported in waves across the desert.

"Jesus," Harry said.

Paul spat sand out of his mouth.

Bob laughed sheepishly. Whatever he had expected when he pressed the trigger of the rifle, the disappearance of the beetle and sand in everyone's face were not it.

Bob carried his father's Weatherby. Paul and Harry each carried a Mossberg .22. Paul's was a gift from his father. His father had given it to him on his twelfth birthday. Paul did not know how Harry had acquired his. Harry's father had died when Harry was small.

The desert was heating up, the sky going from blue to white with the heightening of the sun. Paul had hunted in the desert with his father and his uncle before, though not in this part of it. Here it was only rocks and sand and a little brush. They had not found anything to shoot at except birds and beetles. They had missed the birds they shot at.

The only thing Paul had ever shot, aside from cans and targets, was a bird. Down near Indio with his father and uncle, Paul had sighted on a bird in the distance. He had barely tightened his finger on the trigger when the rifle went

off. It was his new rifle, his Mossberg, and the sensitive trigger had surprised him.

He had shot a hummingbird. Had he taken notice of the
tree it was feeding at, he would have known it was not as far
away as he had thought. He had thought it was a large bird,
but far away. His uncle had been impressed by Paul's eye—to
shoot a hummingbird in flight, something so small—but his
father had said, "Don't you feel bad?"

Paul had felt very bad and, deep inside himself, frightened. He had not shot anything since, though he had wanted to. But he had not seen anything to shoot but birds and
beetles. He felt that if he could kill something larger he
would absolve himself of the first killing. He could tell himself then that the hummingbird was practice for the second,
and necessary. It was difficult to know what to feel about the
hummingbird. Mostly what Paul felt right now was that he
had done something wrong.

Bob was walking in a circle around the point of ground
he had shot into.

"What are you looking for?" Paul said.

"That beetle. The blast may have blown him away somewhere."

"My ears are still ringing," Harry said.

"There's the varmint," Bob said.

It was crawling up what must have been to it a long,
steady hill. It was about four feet from where Bob had shot
at it. It had all of its legs.

"Maybe it isn't the same one," Harry said.

"It doesn't matter. I'll get it this time."

"Don't," Paul said.

"Why not?"

"It's just the waste of a bullet." Paul couldn't think of anything else to say.

Bob smiled quizzically at him. Then he took aim and shot at the beetle.

"Jesus Christ!" Harry said.

They looked for the beetle. It was on its back on top of the small mound. As they watched, it righted itself.

"Let it go," Paul said.

"All right."

"I can hardly hear," said Harry.

".,.," Paul said.

"What?" Harry's face was contorted with the effort to hear.

"All queers are deaf!" Paul shouted.

Bob laughed.

"Let's go back to the car," Paul said.

Bob made that interrogative smile again. "It was a short day."

"We're not going to find anything around here. Not after those two cannon blasts."

"Probably not," Bob said. He pulled back the bolt on the Weatherby. A round flew out of the chamber and landed on the ground. Bob retrieved it. "I wonder how my father does it. They never fly back that way when he opens the bolt."

"We can go down by Indio. I was there with my father once."

"Did you find anything worth shooting?"

"We tracked a mountain lion. But the tracks were probably old."

"Is that the rifle you were carrying?"

"Yeah."

"Good thing you didn't find that mountain lion."

They started back toward the car.

"…," Paul said.

"What?" said Harry.

"All queers are deaf," Paul whispered.

"What did you say?" Harry demanded.

Paul and Bob laughed.

"What's that?" Harry said. "Up there."

There was a dry wash on their right. There was the embankment on the far side and then a rise that climbed away from the dead river to a knoll that gave onto a ridge. On the lip of the ridge, a quarter-mile from the knoll, was a wooden structure.

"It's a house."

"Hell. We've been shooting around it."

Harry cupped his hands around his eyes. "It looks abandoned."

"How can you tell?"

"Because the wood is gray, as though it hasn't been painted in a long time, and a board has been knocked out of the side."

"Let's go up," Paul said.

"Uh-uh. Not me," Harry said.

"Why not?"

"Because it's weird. What's a house doing out here?"

"I'm going to take a look."

Paul started down the embankment into the wash. Bob followed. After a moment Harry followed Bob. Walking toward the knoll, they began to spread out. Paul walked ahead and Bob walked at Paul's right rear and Harry was behind and to the left of both of both of them. On the other side of the knoll the ridge flattened onto a table. The house was ahead of them then, a little to the right. To the left, leading away from the house, was a strip of green-leafed trees, sycamore and eucalyptus, and sparse grass. The green strip broadened until the land began to rise again. Then the grass ended abruptly and the trees at the edge of the rise threw shadows against the loose rock and dirt of another brown hill. Paul moved off to the left into the trees.

"Where are you going?" Harry called after him.

Paul didn't answer. In the trees there was the odor of chlorophyll. The grass grew out of marshy ground that sucked at his boots. Gnats flew in small circles around his face. He came out of the trees where they ended at the edge of the rise, and continued up to the top of the hill.

"Hey! Where are you going?" he heard Harry yell.

The land leveled out again. There, ahead, were the remains of a corral, the rails fallen and gray, cracked with weather and age. Paul walked counterclockwise around the corral. He was almost to the far edge of the circle when he saw something lying in the brush off to his right. It was large and he thought it might get up. When it didn't move, Paul went closer, holding his rifle ready. It was a horse.

Where its eyes had been, there was emptiness. The flesh was desiccated and pulled back from the teeth. The belly gaped open and hollow. It was simply dried flesh, too dried-out to be called meat. Nothing buzzed around it or moved on it. The flies had finished with it. The face did not make any kind of expression, neither a grin nor a sneer. It did not even show indifference.

Moving away from the horse, Paul saw another. It was like the first: no eyes, no stomach. The tongue was gone, too.

Old, Paul thought.

He moved again. Here was a mule. It was like the horses: all the soft parts were gone and the carcass was dried out. As he moved, Paul saw another horse and then another mule, and then other horses and more mules. Soon he understood that he was walking in a circle, the dead horses and mules led him in a circle, and he was returning to the corral.

Standing beside the broken rails, Paul realized that he had not seen any bullet holes in the pelts of the dead animals. What could have killed them? And the spacing between animals was uniform: it took ten to twelve of his steps to get from one to the next. How could it have occurred? There were twenty-eight horses and mules. Could all have been killed at once? Why hadn't any run away? But maybe some had. Maybe some besides these spread through the hills a long time ago. But these formed a complete circle. Where would others have fit in this configuration? Paul did not think any had escaped.

He walked back to the house where Bob and Harry were.

As he approached, he heard the straining of wood and then its breaking, and then he heard a shout. Coming closer, he saw through a tattered wall that Harry was standing up to his waist in the floor. Surprise was still on his face.

Bob said, "Are you all right?"

"Of course I'm all right! What a stupid question! I do this all the time! I always make holes in floors and then jump into them! I wanted to do this!"

Bob laughed.

"Silly boy," Harry said.

The house could never have been much. A room, another room, a sink, a toilet. No doors or windows now. Holes in the walls, now one in the floor. The floor tipped away from higher ground toward the ledge they had seen from below. Magazines and newspapers were everywhere, as though they had been strewn deliberately.

Harry made no effort to climb out of the floor. "Better not come any farther," he told Bob. "I don't think these boards will support you. Hey, look who's here! And where have you been, my fine young fellow?"

"Up there," Paul said.

"Up there? Up there? Come, come, young man. Certainly you can be more precise than that. Precisely where up there, precisely?"

"Do you need a hand?"

"Thanks, but I have two of my own. It was nice of you to ask, though."

Bob laughed.

Harry climbed out of the hole in the floor.

"All of these magazines are mine. You can't have any. Either of you. Because I went through the floor. First one through the floor gets all the magazines. And I'm not going to share them."

"They look old," Bob said.

He and Harry began to sort through those nearest at hand. Paul stood at the doorway and watched.

"Here's one that's only five years old," Harry said. "*Life.* That's the name of the magazine, not a philosophical comment. Actually, it's a philosophical comment as well as the name of this magazine. What's wrong?"

"Nothing," Paul said.

"Ho, ho. Nothing. What is it?"

"I'll show you."

They followed Paul to the corral.

"There," Paul said. "Also to the right. Now farther."

Paul stood by the first horse and directed them until they comprehended that they were following a circle. They continued until they were brought back around to where Paul stood. The three of them then walked back in silence toward the house but didn't stop there. They walked until they were at Paul's car.

"Where to?" Bob asked.

"Not home," Harry said.

"The Salton Sea?" Paul suggested.

"What's at the Salton Sea?"

"We could swim, if nothing else."

"Let's go to the Salton Sea. I'm not ready to go home," Harry said.

"The Salton Sea," Bob agreed.

Paul handed the keys to Harry. "One of you guys drive. I'm going to catch some zees."

Paul did not sleep, though he did not think of the dead horses and mules either. He thought how tired he was and how good it felt to lie down, and that it was amazing that he could lie in such comfort in such a cramped space. The comfort was a luxury and Paul could not get enough of it. As he listened to the nonwords made by the other boys, he began to think about the horses, and then he fell asleep.

He awoke sweating. The car was bouncing over rocks or ruts. He sat up and saw that Harry was pulling off to the side of the highway.

"Where are we?"

"The Salton Sea."

On the opposite side of the road, across the sand and

scrub, was still, steel-blue water.

"Why are we stopped here?"

"We thought we'd get in some shooting before it gets dark," Harry said.

It was mid-afternoon. The terrain on this side of the highway was scrub and rock and, not far off, low rounded hills.

They got out of the car and loaded their rifles.

"Do you think we'll see anything?" Bob asked.

"I think it's still too hot," Paul said.

They walked down the road bank and began watching for the movement of animals.

"I wonder how all these boulders got here," Paul said.

"Flashflood, maybe," Bob said.

"This was all sea bottom once," Harry said. "Maybe they're left from that time."

"I prefer to think it was flashfloods."

"Well, you're wrong. These are obviously sea boulders, left from an ancient time. Nay, a pre-ancient time. Any fool can see that. Fool."

"The only thing to do is wait for the next flashflood and see if any boulders get washed down," Paul said. "Jeez, this is dumb. What the hell are we talking about?"

"I don't know, " Bob said.

"Life. With a capital el," Harry said.

They split up. Harry moved off to the right, Paul to the left, leaving Bob in the center.

Something white flashed. Paul stopped, waited. He didn't see it again. He walked ahead cautiously. He saw her then. The white was her halter. Or brassiere. Halter, probably. She was wearing the halter and a pair of dun-colored shorts. She ran across his line of vision from left to right. Her hair was light brown and she wore white tennis shoes or deck shoes. She ran, it seemed to Paul, with pleasure and grace.

He had not gone far from the highway. He guessed that her parents were camped on the other side, down by the water. He told himself that she had wanted to get away by herself for a while and she had crossed the highway to run beside the low brown hills. Paul could imagine himself falling in love with her but then thought that would be impossible because they had only a little of the afternoon left. He did not envision his love for her, or hers for him, extending into the night.

Paul shouted. The girl was about fifty yards away when she stopped. Paul started toward her. Stepping between a clump of sagebrush and a large boulder, Paul looked down to secure his footing. When he looked up, the girl was gone. Paul looked in every direction. He felt desperation closing on him. He shouted again. She's hiding, he thought. He went to where he had last seen her. She's afraid. He wanted to tell her how mistaken she was to be afraid.

He searched for her, watching for the flash of her halter, until he became convinced that she had returned to her parents' campsite across the highway.

Paul walked back to the car. Soon Bob and Harry came back. They had not seen anything worth shooting at. No one felt like swimming. They might as well go home.

Paul wanted to ask if they had heard him shout, but as they did not mention it, he did not either.

Bob drove. Paul sat in the back. The wind was hot coming through the car windows. It was pleasant to feel it, knowing they were going back to the colder wind of the coast.

On the freeway they came alongside a bus from a Catholic school. It was filled with girls. Harry pulled his pants down and stuck his ass out the window and Bob beeped the horn. The girls clapped their hands and shouted encouragement. Paul laughed, but when he had finished laughing it was as though there had never been anything funny in the world.

JOHN

The Buddy Rich-Gene Krupa duel had finished and now Paul and Harry were listening to the Kingston Trio on the stereo. Paul preferred the great drummers tonight but Harry wanted the sad harmony of "Tom Dooley." Harry's stepfather had just walked out on Harry's mother.

"You should listen to *Sketches of Spain* if you want to really feel bad," Paul said.

"No," Harry said.

"Have you heard it?"

"No, but I don't want to feel that bad. This is bad enough for me." He sang with the song until it was over.

"I'll get us something to eat," he said. Paul sat on the bed and read album jackets until Harry returned.

Harry brought back a plate of bacon and a bowl of lettuce. He set the plate and the bowl on the bed and took a salt shaker out of his shirt pocket.

"Do you like salt on your lettuce?"

"Sure," Paul said.

Harry shook salt over the lettuce.

Paul hadn't had this snack before. He liked the combination of the aromatic bacon and the crispy lettuce.

Harry put the dishes on the floor. "I'll take them into the kitchen later. My aunt is in there with her boyfriend. The slut."

Harry lived now in a house filled with women. There were his mother, his aunt, their mother and his sister.

"I like your aunt," Paul said.

"Her boyfriend's probably porking her on the kitchen table. I was watching television one night last week and they came into the living room and started groping each other right there on the sofa in front of me."

"Nice of them to let you watch."

"He's not the only one she screws. She's got another boyfriend. Both of them are cops."

"That might come in handy someday, having an aunt who knows cops."

"Yeah. If only she weren't a slut about it. I'm going to put the Kingston Trio on again. If you mind, say so."

"No, they're okay."

"Did my mother tell you about her mistake at the newspaper?"

"No. What happened?"

"Some church or other had just been built and the paper printed a press release about it. But instead of writing 'the house that God built,' Mother wrote 'the house that John built.'"

John was the name of Harry's stepfather. Paul laughed.

Harry said, "The neighbors came over and accused me of ruining their lawn."

"What did you tell them?"

"They didn't talk to me. They talked to my mother. I told her I didn't do it."

"Did she believe you?"

"I doubt it."

Three nights before, Harry and Paul had poured gasoline

on Harry's neighbors' lawn. They were close friends of Harry's stepfather. In conversation with other neighbors, they had referred to Harry's mother as a barfly.

"The hell with them," Paul said. "They can't prove anything."

"I could go over there and admit that I did it. Maybe that slob would hit me."

"Striking a minor."

"Yeah."

"He goes to jail and your mother pays a fine because you destroyed their property."

"Going to jail is worse. He has a family to support. They count on him to stay out of jail."

"But your mother would still have to pay the fine."

"Yeah."

"Maybe he wouldn't hit you. Then your mother would have to pay a fine and he wouldn't go to jail."

"Maybe I wouldn't have to admit doing anything. Maybe I could get him to hit me anyway."

"Forget it. He might hurt you."

"It would be worth it."

"No it wouldn't."

"Okay. It was a dumb idea."

"I'm not tired. Are you?"

"No. I haven't been sleeping much lately. But I'm not tired."

"Let's go down to the Denny's and get a cup of coffee."

"What time do you think it is?"

"Two, three."

"What the hell. Let's go."

Outside, the air was heavy and warm and filled with the

fumes of the past evening's traffic. The lights from the gas station and the Denny's and the supermarket two blocks away made the night seem almost like day.

Walking past the elementary school, Harry wanted to stop to play on the swings. After a few minutes Harry got off the swing. "I wish somebody would just push the damn button," he said.

There was an empty lot where there had been a Baptist church. A McDonald's was going to go up where the church had been—so Paul's father had heard—but for now there was just an empty lot.

At the gas station, Harry said, "I have to take a leak."

He walked past a guy buttoning his fly in front of the men's room door. The guy swayed from side to side as he managed the buttons. Going by him, Paul said, "Had a little too much, huh?" and immediately could have kicked himself.

The drunk guy said, "What? Hey!"

Paul continued walking. Another guy whose eyes were clearer than the first guy's was coming out of the bathroom as Paul went in. This guy said, "What's going on?"

Paul locked the door. Harry was staring at him.

"Why did you say that?"

"Hell, I don't know."

"Jesus Christ. Didn't you see their motorcycles? And they're wearing colors. They're part of a gang, man."

"I didn't see any motorcycles."

"By the pumps. There were two other guys with them. They were getting gas."

"How do you know they're together?"

"They're together, man."

Someone knocked on the door.

Paul and Harry cautioned each other with their eyes not to say anything. The doorknob turned, then stopped where the lock blocked it.

The knock at the door came again. "Hey! Is somebody in there? I gotta piss!"

The knob twisted, then rattled violently. "Hey! I gotta piss! Let me in!"

"Maybe he really does have to piss," Harry said.

"They just got through pissing when we got here."

"I hear you talking in there!"

"I'm taking a leak," Harry shouted.

"That's a long leak, man."

Harry went to the toilet and began to pee.

"Okay, man," said the voice from outside. "I hear you." The voice made a kind of giggle.

Harry buttoned his Levis. He didn't flush. After a minute the voice outside called, "Hey, man, you took your leak. Let me in."

"I'm on the can, man!" Harry called back.

"He says he's on the can," Paul and Harry heard the voice say.

"He ain't on the can," another voice said.

"Hey in there!" this voice called. It was a heavier, more self-assured voice than the first one. "Hey! You hear me?"

"What do you want, man? I'm on the can!" Harry shouted.

"You ain't on no can," the second voice said. "Open this damn door now."

Harry shook his head for no.

"Open this door, damnit." It was as though the voice had

seen Harry's movements through the door.

There was a *whump!* against the outside of the door and it shook and rattled as though it had been hit. The *whump!* came again. Then the second voice said, "Open this door, man, before I get mad." Then, after twenty or thirty seconds had passed, the *whump!* came again.

The second voice said, "My shoulder's getting sore," and it and another voice laughed. Then there were two more *whump!*s and the second voice yelled, "I'm getting mad, man! You'd better open this fuckin' door!" *Whump! Whump!* At this last there was the additional sound of cracking wood.

"You're gettin' it, man," said the first voice or a third one.

"Fuck you, I'm gettin' it. You try it."

There was another assault on the door but the cracking sound was not repeated. Then, for half a minute or a minute, there wasn't any sound at all.

A voice said, "All right, man, we're going." Paul and Harry could hear a motorcycle revving behind the voice. "You guys hear me? I said we're going. It's safe to come out now, we're going. All right. Stay in there. I'm going. You guys take it easy."

From outside then, there was silence. There was not the sound of footsteps diminishing with distance, there was not the whisper of voices conspiring.

Then there was the squeal, as of a pig being gutted while alive, of a motorcycle peeling out, and then the *rrrr'uv!rrr* of the gear change and the gain in speed.

"Maybe they really left," Harry said softly.

"How many cycles did you see?"

"Two."

"Only one left. And he's only gone around the block."

"I'm going to take a look."

"No!"

Before Harry could open the door, one of the voices from outside said, "I hear you in there, man. You'd better open this door."

"Fuck you!" Harry yelled.

"Whoo! Listen to that! You're gonna be sorry you said that, man. We're some bad hombres. We're wanted by the cops in four states."

Silence, for a moment only.

"If you come out now, we won't make it too bad on you. But if we have to come in there after you, you're gonna wish you'd come out when we gave you the chance. So make up your minds."

"Fuck you, asshole!"

"Okay, man, you asked for it."

Paul and Harry watched the knob turn. It turned all the way and the door began to open.

"They got the key!" Harry screamed. Then the door was closed again, Paul's and Harry's bodies from palm of hand to ball of foot in linear rigidity opposing the pressure on the door to open. Paul felt the muscles in his back cording, trying to pop out of the encasing skin, it seemed, and he saw the agony on Harry's face beside his own, and heard his own voice yelling, "Lock it! Lock the door!" and Harry's yelling back, "They have the key! They'll just open it again!" and felt the door in fact pressing, pressing open, only an inch and then closing again, and heard then Harry's "Oh God!" Harry's back to the door now, the muscular energy running from heel to shoulder, not as effective, not nearly as effective, Paul knew, as making yourself into that single ungiving steel-hard bunch-muscled line from palm to shoulder to back to leg regardless of the pain, think about something besides the pain, think about nothing at all, but don't bend, just don't bend… "Turn around," Paul hissed, "turn around, they're getting the door open."

Harry spun and came into that magical steel line again, and again the door closed. They sensed that there was no resistance now, no one opposing them. Paul locked the door. The knob didn't turn.

"Oh God," Harry said, breathless now, the words coming out in a whisper. Then he said, "Maybe this time they'll leave."

"No. It's another trick," Paul said. He knew.

"We can't stay in here forever. Sooner or later they'll have to leave," Harry said.

"We can hold out till dawn. If we have to. Maybe the attendant will call the cops before then."

"The attendant gave them the key. He's not going to call the cops. And what makes you think they'll go away when it gets light? Do you think they're vampires?"

"People will be stopping to get gas on their way to work. These guys won't try anything then."

"Tomorrow is Sunday. No work."

"Church, then. People will be going to church."

"At eight, nine. Stopping for gas around seven, seven-thirty. It must be four or five now. All right. We can hold out."

"We can't let ourselves relax like this. They could unlock the door and be in here before we can react. We have to keep pressure on the door so we have some warning when they come back. We can take turns pushing against it."

"God. All right. I'll take it first."

Harry angled himself at forty-five degrees against the door. "I can't. My back won't take any more."

"I'll do it."

Paul took up the same angle as Harry had. Paul's back ached. He told himself he could think past the ache, put himself on the other side of the pain where there was nothing, but he was so tired now and the ache was so general, not only in his back but in his arms and shoulders and legs and even his stomach, he felt them all now, that he couldn't gather his concentration, and in a moment he found himself leaning against the door, the door serving to prevent his falling forward rather than he serving to obstruct the door's opening.

"This isn't going to work." Paul stood erect, turned and leaned back against the door.

"Maybe they're gone," Harry said.

"They haven't gone."

The door sprang open, throwing Paul against the far wall. He hit it with his hands, pivoted and threw himself at the door. Harry was already on it. But this time it was different: the end of a two-by-four protruded into the room between the door and the frame and Paul knew even before he felt his strength peak that he and Harry would not get the door closed again and that they were using themselves up while those on the other side of the door were saving their own strength.

Now Harry shoved away from the door, back-pedaling to the rear wall. Before Paul could shout—he had the words already formed to say: What the hell are you doing!—the door came open for good, fixing Paul to the wall behind it. He had the sense of Harry lunging toward the open doorway. Then there was a tremendous *crackl*ing and Harry howled once, the sound ripped from him with no chance to suppress it, and he shot back against the rear wall and fell in a pile to the floor, all knees and elbows, his face tucked inside his forearms.

Two guys came in after him. They were not that big really, but they moved with a certainty and coordination that Paul knew he and Harry did not have. The one in front picked Harry up by his shirt and his hair, Harry yelling, "Haven't you done enough!" and bounced his face off the rim of the toilet. Harry howled again but the sound coming out of him had something of calculation in it, as though he understood now what was expected of him and was providing it.

The guy who was not busy with Harry said, "Where's the other one?"

Paul pushed the door away and stepped out from the wall. "Here I am."

The guy was shorter than Paul, but stocky. He was older than Paul had thought, looking at him from the rear, mid-twenties maybe. He had sandy hair. He punched with his right and Paul blocked it. Surprise came over the guy's face, then determination. He used both fists alternately now, going for the face with every punch. Paul caught the rhythm and rolled his shoulders with it and used his forearms to deflect the guy's hands. There was an instant's hesitation and Paul, knowing what was coming, brought his leg up and the guy's knee glanced off Paul's thigh.

Paul was enjoying this, the guy's frustration. Soon the guy dropped one of his hands and Paul hit him in the throat, knowing that he had done something stupid. And now the

guy came in again, and came in with a gut punch and Paul
buckled but knew then that the guy would kick him and he
stood up, twisting his hip to catch the knee or foot, and then
they stood, staring at each other.

The guy who had been pounding Harry came up and
said, "Come on." Then he punched Paul. He was a lot faster
than the guy Paul had been occupied with and he was very
strong. The punch opened Paul's eyebrow and slammed him
back against the wall. Paul went down. He waited for the
kick, but the one who had hit him said, "Let's go," and the
two walked out.

As soon as they had gone, Harry rushed across the room
and closed and locked the door. Outside, motorcycles revved
and then were gone. Harry looked in the mirror. "Goddamnit! Look at me! Look at all this blood! Jesus Christ!"

He turned on the tap and washed his face. "Jesus Christ!
Look at this blood!"

He did not look so bad now that the blood was washed
off. Just a cut in the center of his forehead. Paul had seen
worse. He wondered how Harry had got off so lightly.

Paul took Harry's place at the sink. There was not too
much blood; it was coagulating around the hairs of his eyebrow. Harry had a wad of toilet paper pressed against his
forehead. He handed another wad to Paul. Paul took it and
put it to his eyebrow. Paul wondered how Harry could have
been hit with the two-by-four and had his face smacked on
the toilet bowl and come out of it with only one cut on his
forehead. Paul would have to ask him about it. Someday.

"Where's that attendant?" Harry said. He opened the
door. The gray-blue light of dawn had replaced the black of
night. There was traffic. A car waited at the corner for the

light to change; another barreled through the intersection.

A thin man wearing a bill cap with the corporate logo of the service station emblazoned on it came over to them. He pushed the cap back on the crown of his head and Paul saw that he was going bald. "What's going on here?" he demanded.

Harry shoved him. "You son of a bitch! You gave them the key!"

"Harry," Paul said.

"Don't you push me! I'll call the police!" the attendant threatened.

"Call the police! Why didn't you call them before, you son of a bitch! You bastard! Why did you give those other bastards the key! Look what they did to me!"

"Leave me alone! I'll call the police!"

"Harry."

"Call them! Call them! I'll call them! Son of a bitchin' bastard cocksucker! Where's that board! Call them, son of a bitch! Call them before I use this board on you!"

"I'll call the police. Don't you hit me. Look at this mess you made in here. Who's going to clean this up?"

Harry made a funny sound. Then this sound began to alternate with another sound that was coming out of him. At first Paul thought that Harry was crying, but then he seemed to be laughing. Harry fell down on the ground, crying or laughing or crying and laughing. From the ground, Harry pointed up at the station attendant: "Look! Look at the son of a bitch's name! Look on his shirt!" and went on making those sounds and gasping for breath.

Embroidered in script on the right breast of the attendant's shirt was the name "John."

"Oh, oh," Harry gasped. "You son of a bitch. Look what you did to me, you son of a bitch."

CONCEALMENTS

Harry said he'd seen the guy sitting on the curb there by the bench where the bus stopped on Beach Boulevard. The guy wasn't drunk but he wanted to be, he said, and panhandled Harry for his change and then asked him to point out the nearest bar. The guy said that his best friend had been killed in Korea. He died in my arms, the guy said, and that's why I drink. Harry had pointed the guy to the Blue Moon Tavern and that was the last Harry saw of him. But he'd left Harry his name on a slip of paper and said he lived in L.A. and if Harry ever went to Los Angeles he should call him. Harry had lost the slip of paper.

"It's a common name," Harry said.

"Smith? Jones? Green? Brown?" Paul suggested.

"Brown, I think. What's the difference?"

"Let's go find him."

"What? Why?"

"I want to know about the war. Maybe he can tell us something."

"How will we find him?"

"We'll go to L.A., stop at a phone booth, and look up his name."

"There are a lot of Browns in the phone book," Sara said. She brought them each a cup of coffee and set milk and sugar on the table. Like a waitress, Paul thought. Or a little mother.

"Do you know his first name?" he asked Harry.

"He told it to me but I don't remember it. It was probably on that slip of paper."

"Would you remember it if you heard it again?"

"I don't know."

"Was it a common name too?"

"I don't know. I don't remember."

"I don't know. I don't remember. You'll never make me talk," Sara said.

Harry laughed. When he laughed his eyes glistened and his skin flushed, as though in delight with or appreciation of what Sara had said.

Sara sipped her coffee. It was mostly milk, the way children have coffee.

"I think we ought to go to L.A. and find this guy. What was he doing out here anyway, did he say?" Paul said.

"I think he said, but I don't remember," Harry said. He and Sara laughed.

"He took the bus out here," Harry said, and laughed again. The laughter this time was not in response to Sara but was an attempt to reinforce his own wit, and his face did not redden or do the things it did when Sara was funny.

"Let's go to L.A.," Paul said. "I have my folks' car for the afternoon."

"We won't be able to find him, Paul," Harry said.

"That isn't why he wants to go," Sara said.

"Why do I want to go, then?"

"I don't know. Maybe you just want to go to L.A."

"So what are we going to do? Go into L.A., stop at a couple of phone booths and then come home?" Harry said.

"We'll find him. Brown. Let's go."

"I have to be home at seven," Sara said.

In the car Paul studied the map. The part of L.A. that was closest to where they lived was East L.A. Paul decided to go there.

"Why there? That's Mexican, man," Harry said.

"So?"

"So they'll make tacos out of us."

"No they won't."

"Sir, you jest."

"Maybe we should just ask Telephone Information," Sara said.

"I'm going to East L.A. to find this Brown. If you don't want to go, then don't."

"I don't think we should take Sara," Harry said.

"If you're going, I'll go with you," Sara said. Paul didn't know which of them she had directed this to. It could be either of us or both of us, Paul thought, that's the beauty of it.

They drove into East L.A. The houses were painted in pastels. There were a lot of little grocery stores, not so many supermarkets. Not everybody, but most people, were brown.

Paul stopped the car at a service station that had a phone booth at the corner of its lot.

There were four pages of Browns in the first directory Paul looked at. This directory covered L.A., but not East L.A. There was a second directory for East L.A. In this directory there was only a column and a half of Browns. Also, Paul discovered from reading the first pages of the L.A. directory, Los Angeles was divided into telephone exchanges and each exchange had its own sub-directory within the larger directory; you had to know where in L.A. you wanted to call before you could even ask Information for assistance. And, depending on the proximity of the exchanges, you could be charged for a long distance call if you dialed one exchange from another.

Paul went back to the car.

"Did you find him?" Harry said. He was smirking.

"Did that guy Brown write his address on that piece of paper he gave you?" It was all Paul could think of to say.

"No," Harry said. "Uh-uh. No sir. He did not. May I ask why you ask, sir?"

"No. You may not."

Paul started the car. Sara, sitting beside him, was turned so that with a slight shift of her head she could look at either Paul or Harry. That's the beauty of it, Paul thought, she might or might not be looking at either of us, and neither of us would know.

It was getting dark. Sara's arm hung down over the back of her seat. Paul knew that Harry was holding Sara's hand. He felt himself grin.

"What's funny?" Sara asked.

"Nothing."

"Then why are you smiling?"

"I don't know."

"Jesus."

"May I ask where we're going?" Harry said.

"Home. Now do me a favor and shut up."

Sara turned in her seat so that she faced out the windshield. From the back where Harry was, there was no sound.

In Fullerton they stopped at the Denny's on Orangethorpe. It was seven-thirty. Sara went to the pay phone to call her mother. Paul and Harry had nothing to say to each other. When Sara returned she sat down next to Paul.

Harry ordered fries and a coke, Sara ordered a coke and chili with oyster crackers, and Paul had coffee and a cheeseburger. None of them were hungry, but they had not eaten all day.

Sara said she had to get home after they finished eating, her mother was angry with her. Harry said something and after a while Paul said something about the horses in the desert, describing them, how they had looked. Sara put her spoon down so that it clattered on the table. She slid out of the booth and ran outside. Customers' heads turned as she ran by them.

"That really isn't the sort of thing one talks about at dinner, old chap," Harry said. He wiped his mouth with a paper napkin, then wadded it and dropped it on his plate. He put money on the table, then slid out of the booth and went outside.

Paul sipped his coffee until it was gone. He accepted another half cup from the waitress.

Harry came back inside. "Sara has to get home."

Paul paid the bill, then went out. Harry and Sara were standing by the car.

"Why did you run away?" Paul said. He unlocked the Volkswagen doors.

"I got sick. Did you have to start talking about those horses again while I was eating? It was enough to gag a maggot," Sara said.

Harry laughed.

"If you were sick, why didn't you go into the bathroom? It was closer."

"I didn't think of it. If you don't believe me, I'll show you

where I vomited. Do you want to see it? I left a little puddle
in the alley."

"Sure. I'll look."

"Oh, for Christ's sake. Take us home," Harry said.

After they dropped Sara off, Paul drove to Harry's house
and parked at the curb. He thought about punching Harry.

Harry said, "I never thought I'd say this to you, Paul,
but I have to tell you that I'm ashamed to consider you my
friend. You were disgusting. Dragging us to East L.A.—I'll
bet you still don't know why you did it. Talking about those
goddamned horses while we were trying to eat…"

It's Sara, Paul thought. He wants Sara. All the rest is just
to conceal what's really going on.

"…I was really disgusted," Harry was repeating.

"Get out of the car," Paul said.

Harry stopped talking. He seemed surprised. He seemed
to be waiting for something.

"Get out or I'll kick your ass," Paul said.

Harry opened the car door. He laughed as he got out.
The laughter may have been real or it may have been fake.
He started to say something.

The engine turned over and Paul slipped the gearshift
lever into first. He eased off the clutch and the car moved
away from the curb. The passenger door was open and Harry
was still trying to say something as Paul pulled away. Paul
reached over and closed the door.

There were things Paul would have liked to know. He
would have liked Harry to tell him what he had hoped to
accomplish when he tried to break past those guys who had
penned them up in that gas station restroom. Paul would
have liked Harry to tell him whether he realized that he

would be leaving him, Paul, to take them on alone. Paul
would have liked Harry to tell him this.

Maybe it isn't Sara, Paul thought. Maybe it's something
else altogether that Sara conceals. Sara as an idea, not as a person. We have to distinguish between the two, Paul thought.

And what about me? When they had him down, could I
have come out from behind the door any sooner than I did?

And I want Sara, too.

Thinking about it, Paul decided that he would have to
ask himself someday why he had wanted to go to L.A. He
would have to make it a point to ask himself about that
someday when he thought he knew the answer.

PAUL AND SARA, THEIR CHILDHOOD

I

"Then why does she call you 'Jim'?"

"I don't know. Ask her. She likes the sound of it better. She's like that."

"Oh, she's like *that*."

"That's enough, okay? I don't want to talk about her anymore."

"Yah. Vatever you say, sveetie."

Paul wished Dennis would stop talking like that, like a television German. Ever since Dennis started college he had been talking like that. Sveetie. Yah. Vatever. Whatever Dennis was discovering, Paul did not think it had anything to do with television Germans. Plus, Paul did not like Dennis to patronize him, and that was exactly what Dennis was doing whenever he put on that phony accent.

"Look."

"What?"

Across the street a fat Mexican was standing over a blond guy who was lying on the sidewalk. The Mexican was saying something and motioning for the blond guy to get up. The American stood up and started to back away.

"'Ey. Com'ere," the Mexican said. The American walked over to him. When he was within punching distance, the Mexican knocked him down.

"Com'on. Com'ere," the Mexican said. He gestured for the American to stand up again. The American began slowly to get up. A policeman watched from the corner of the street.

"Com'ere."

Paul could see that the scalp at the back of the American's head had been torn. It was puckered and pink and looked like a cat's ass.

The Mexican swung and the American fell back over the hood of a parked car. The Mexican swung again and the American rolled away. He disappeared in the crowd that had congregated.

"Com'ere," the Mexican called after him, but not very loudly, as though he were tired of hitting him and hoped that he would not come back.

Seeing that between the Mexican and the blond guy put Paul in a better mood. He and Dennis would have something now to which they could refer esoterically. "'Ey. Com'ere," Paul would say, and Dennis would laugh at the scene it conjured up.

"Hey, did you really think you stopped the ocean?" Dennis asked.

"I *did* stop it."

"What did it feel like?"

"It felt good. But it scared the hell out of me."

"But I mean, what were you thinking? What were you saying to yourself to make it stop?"

"I just said 'Stop' and it stopped. The waves did."

"Oh wow. That was some strong dope. I should have tried to do that."

"Yeah, but it sure scared the hell out of me. I had to tell

them to come on in before they started breaking again."

"That's great," Dennis said.

Coming out of the nightclub, Dennis said, "You ought to loosen up."

"Yeah, I know."

"She was only trying to help you."

"I know."

Paul felt terrible. Thinking about what had happened, or rather what hadn't happened, he decided that he had not been drunk enough. What he needed was to get drunk enough to be able to do what he wanted to do.

"Let's go in that place across the street," he said.

"You know, I climaxed at the same time as that girl on the stage did."

"Let's cross here."

"The girl who was jerking me off was sure surprised. I guess she wasn't expecting me to come."

"Was she angry? She looked angry."

"She wanted me to give her ten dollars. She said that's what it would have cost if we'd gone in the back. I told her to go to hell." Dennis laughed. "I got a free hand job."

"You sure got drunk again fast," Dennis said.

"Yeah. But I keep losing it. As soon as I start walking I get sober again. Oops!"

"Okay, sober. Watch out you don't fall through that shop window."

"My head is sober but my legs are drunk."

"Hey, what did that girl say to you when we walked in?"

"When we walked in? When she was whispering?"

"Yes."

"She wanted to know if I sixty-nined."

Dennis laughed. "You sure told her."

"What did I say?"

"You said, 'Sure, baby, I sixty-nine all over the place.'"

"Christ. Was I that loud?"

"You were pretty loud."

"Christ. No wonder she looked embarrassed. Did I really say that?"

"Maybe you said 'all the time' instead of 'all over the place.' She got the point anyway."

"Oh, God."

"I thought it was cool."

Crap, thought Paul.

"Vat's zis?"

Spilling onto the street, another crowd had collected around a tall kid whose mouth was bleeding. His shoulders rolled forward, his legs bent slightly at the knees, his fists clenched but held low at the waist, the kid faced the crowd in a brawler's imitation of a boxer's crouch. Behind him a display window was smashed out of a storefront.

"'Ey, mate. This shop don't sell pussy. You've got to go down a block for it," a young man with what Paul took to be a British street accent called out. "Red Rosey's the place. It ain't much but it's the best they've got in this fookin' 'ole." The young man was tall and soft-looking, with fair skin and very yellow hair—Paul had never seen hair that was actually yellow before—who was not as drunk as he was pretending to be. Seeing that he had captured Paul's attention, he went

on: "All the way from Panama, mates been sayin', 'Wait'll
you see what's in Tijuana, you'll fook yourself blind in Tijuana.' Shit. This place don't compare to Hamburg. Fat juicy
Nazi girls they've got in Hamburg. These blokes don't know
no better 'n this."

"Here comes the fuzz," a college kid in the crowd said.

"Poli-cee," said a girl who seemed to be with him. Another girl who was in the same faction laughed.

Two cops in uniform and a man in a gray suit with blue
and red threading got out of a patrol car at the curb and
pushed through the aggregation of North Americans to the
kid in front of the broken window. When they got to him
the kid seemed to relax. He straightened up and dabbed
at the blood on his mouth with the back of his hand. The
two uniformed cops took him by the elbows and led him
to the patrol car. The kid didn't resist. The man in the gray
suit stayed behind and surveyed the damage to the window.
Then he turned around and began waving his arms. "Break
it up, break it up," he directed the crowd. Just like on American television. Broderick Crawford, Paul thought.

"That's all she wrote," said one of the college kids.

"Ve-ry in-ter-es-ting," Dennis said. "Should we go to Red
Rosey's?"

"Why don't you go? I think I'll go up this way."

"We could go to the Blue Fox," Dennis said. He was hurt.

"I'd just like to be alone for a while, Dennis. Why don't
we meet, say, at the Blue Fox in about an hour? How about
that?" Oh, Christ, Paul thought, despising himself for being
so condescending.

"Okay. Maybe I'll smoke some dope." Paul could see the
pain behind Dennis' forced smile. In that instant he hated

Dennis. ·

"Just do it where you won't get caught." Paul made himself laugh.

Dennis motioned with his hand, a wave of dismissal or goodbye, and walked off in the direction opposite the one Paul intended to go. Shit, thought Paul.

There was a lot of cigarette smoke in the club but there were not many customers. Most of the whores sat clustered together at the end of the bar. A very fat whore with a large nose and a mole on her cheek came over to the table where Paul was sitting. He shook his head and she turned away and went back to talk with the other whores. After a few moments one with bleached hair and who was not so fat approached him.

"Do you have a cigarette?"

"Sure." Paul lit it for her.

"Thank you." She began to walk away.

"May I buy you a drink?"

The bartender brought her a drink in a small glass and Paul a Tres Equis. Paul knew that the girl's drink was cold tea. He paid the bartender.

"What is your name?" Paul asked.

"Maria."

"Maria. That is a very pretty name."

"What is your name?"

"Paul. Pablo, in Spanish."

"Pablo. That is very nice." Maria patted his hand. He interlaced his fingers with hers and held them. Their hands rested together on the table. Sometimes he squeezed her hand. When he did this she squeezed back.

"You're very pretty, Maria."

"Thank you."

"Do you have a lover, Maria?"

Paul had read in a magazine that whores had lovers, favorites for whom they saved things they would not give to other men.

Maria hesitated before answering. She seemed uncertain and looked at Paul closely. At last she said, "No. I have lived here only six months." She smiled a little.

"Six months?"

She corrected herself. "Six weeks."

"Oh. Where are you from, then?"

"All over. Acapulco, Mexico City, Guadalajara, Cuernevaca, La Paz. Now Tijuana."

Paul smiled. It had not occurred to him that Mexicans might travel much within their own country. He had envisioned Mexicans as living in villages unless something horrible befell their lives, in which case they might move to a city. He had not seen them as volitional.

"You are from San Diego?"

"No. Do you know where Disneyland is? I am from near there. Why did you say San Diego?"

"You look like a Greek. There are too many Greeks in San Diego."

Paul thought she meant "very many" instead of "too many" Greeks. He kept himself from laughing.

"Yes, there are," he said. Then he laughed, and she laughed too. Afterward, he looked at her and smiled. When she returned the smile Paul thought it was in recognition of their collusion in playing the game with the Greeks.

"How much money do you have?"

"Seven and a half dollars." Paul looked in his wallet. "Yes, that's how much."

"Don't you have a friend who would give you money?"

"I came with a friend but I don't know where he is now. How much do I need?"

"Twelve dollars."

"Twelve?"

"Ten dollars for me and the room costs two dollars."

"I don't have it. Do you want to see my wallet?"

"No. I believe you."

She was not looking at him. She was looking across the room toward where the other whores sat. Paul did not want to look at her. He was ashamed because he wanted her and he did not have the money.

Maria turned to him. "Do you want to come with me now?"

"But I don't have the money."

"I will pay for the room."

Paul was very pleased.

Paul sat on the bed watching her undress. He liked her and he liked the room, its odor of recent copulations. He liked its being sordid.

"Aren't you going to take off your clothes?"

She was wearing only her corset and brassiere now. She wasn't wearing panties. He was very excited.

"Yes," he said. His throat was thick and the word hardly came out. Maria unbuttoned his shirt and then helped him with his pants. His shorts were already wet.

"Take those off," he said.

She took off the lace corset, then the brassiere. Then she

lay back on the bed and watched him look at her.

"Be careful not to touch my hair, okay?" It was in a kind of beehive. Paul guessed that it was heavily lacquered because not a bit of it was out of place.

"Okay."

"Don't touch my hair."

"I won't."

He pressed his face into her. At his touch her legs parted. After a moment she said, "Like this." She took his finger; her tongue darted over it in light quick stabs. "Like you did my breast."

He did it and she said, "Yes, like that." After a while they changed positions "so I can come too," Maria said. She reached behind her and spread herself open with her hands. Then they changed positions again and then he was inside her, growing and growing, it was a pleasure beyond a pleasure, so sweet was it, and then before he was ready for it to end it was over, and there were only the two of them in the room on the bed.

"See?" she said. "We came at the same time." Paul did not remember her coming, and thought she must not have.

There was a knock on the door. Paul sat up, frightened.

"Not yet," Maria called.

A woman's voice on the other side of the door said something at length in Spanish.

Maria answered curtly.

Then from the other side of the door the woman shouted in English, "Ai-i-i, you baby! Can't you hold it!"

Maria laughed. Paul was surprised at how resonant her laugh was. It was as though her laugh were entirely independent of the rest of her, at least the part of her he knew, or thought he knew.

"We have to go," she said. She got up and started to put her clothes on. "That was my friend. Did you understand what she said?"

"No."

"She said that the boy who is with her had it up good and hard. She was afraid that he was going to spill his milk before she could find a bed." Maria laughed again, the same laugh but not so loud. "That was very funny," she said. "Get dressed now. We have to leave."

Paul found his shorts.

"Will you wait for me?" She had most of her clothes on now. "Wait for me in the bar." She went out of the room.

Paul hurried to dress. When he had his clothes on he opened the door and looked outside. A whore was holding the skirt of her dress out away from her legs while she scolded a boy, older than Paul, who was leaning against the wall. "You big baby. Can't you control yourself?" The kid's cock was still poking its head outside his fly. It seemed in the dim light still to be wet. The kid looked sullenly at Paul.

Paul didn't see Maria in the bar. As he was walking out he turned and saw the bartender giving him a funny look. Paul walked quickly into the crowd on the sidewalk. When he was halfway down the block he turned once more and saw the bartender standing in the doorway, watching him.

In the car Paul said he wanted to stop for pancakes at a certain restaurant outside of San Diego. When they came to the restaurant Dennis slowed, and Paul thought they would be turning in. But then Dennis jammed it and they sped past the turnoff.

Paul did not think about Dennis now. He felt disgusted with himself about Maria. He felt a double disgust, because he had gone with her in the first place, and then because he had run away from her. At first he thought he felt bad because of the sex part of it, but then he knew that had nothing to do with it. After a while, riding in the car with the memory of her in detail in his mind, he began to get excited again and he felt better about himself.

Finally he fell asleep dreaming about when he and Harry and Bob Ripley found the horses in the desert.

II

Paul reached for her as soon as she let him in but Sara pulled back. She turned away from him.

"I'm ugly," she said.

"What do you mean?"

"I'm ugly, that's all. I don't want you to see me."

"Why not?"

"'Why not?' 'Why not?'" Sara mimicked. "Because I'm ugly."

Paul put his arms around her. She seemed so small, almost as though she weren't there.

"Please," he said.

"Please don't."

"Yes. I want to."

"My mother is in the kitchen."

"She's not listening."

"Yes she is. But it doesn't matter."

She rested against him. Paul could feel her body softening as the tension eased.

"Why don't you ever call me 'little one'?"

"Would you like me to?"

"Yes."

"Why?"

"I've always wanted someone to call me 'little one'."

"Little one."

"Say it again."

"Little one." He said it softer this time. Her face was against his chest and he could feel her flush.

"I love you," he said.

"I don't believe you."

"I love you. I love you," Paul said in a child's voice, teasing her.

"I believe you, but you must tell me you love me more often because sometimes I start to get afraid and I need reassuring."

"What are you afraid of?"

"Of you. That you'll leave me."

"You don't have to be afraid of me. I'll never leave you."

"I am, though. Sometimes. You'll always protect me, won't you, Jimmy?"

"Yes."

"Say it. Please say it. Say you'll always protect me."

"I'll always protect you."

"Oh God, Jim, I need you."

"I'll always be here."

"No, you won't, Jimmy. One day I'll need you and you won't be here."

"Yes I will. I'll always be here."

"I'll be good to you, Jimmy. I'll make myself small and put myself in your pocket and I'll do whatever you want me to do."

"Yes."

"Whenever you want me all you'll have to do is pick me up out of your pocket and I'll be there."

"Yes."

"Tell me I'm your little one, Jimmy."

"My little one."

"I am, you know. I'm only a little girl and I need you to protect me from the wolves in the forest."

"I know."

He held her, waiting for her to say something more. Finally he asked, "Are you afraid of me now?"

"No. Not now. I believe that you love me now."

"I do love you. I love you forever."

"I know you do. Jimmy?"

"Yes?"

"Don't tell me what you did in Tijuana, all right?"

"I wouldn't," Paul said.

"I know you say you wouldn't but sometimes—sometimes you can be cruel. I know you don't mean to be—"

"All right."

"Say that you love me."

"I love you," he said.

"Let's go out tonight, Jimbo. Take me to the drive-in. We'll neck."

"All right. I like to neck with you."

"I love you too, Jimbo."

Walking home, Paul thought about how it was the first time he went out with Sara. They went to the beach where the jetty separated Newport from the Balboa Channel. That area was called The Wedge now. A year ago it did not have a name because nobody went there but surf fishermen and Sara and him that first time. They had raced the length of the jetty and she had won. She had more courage on the rocks than he and her feet were surer. Later he went into the water. She was on her period, she said, she would watch. He caught the first wave only a few yards out and watched, unbelieving, as the water beneath the curl receded, showing the sand pack as hard and ungiving as concrete. The wave drove him down like a steam hammer against a pile, and the sand bounced him back into it. He rolled with it up the beach, confused and directionless, the white moil everywhere above and beneath him, sucking him out now so that it took all of his breath and effort to find the bottom and brace himself against the backrush of water. He rode with the foam of the next wave as high up the beach as he could, turned and sat back against its pull, gulped air and waited for the draw of the wave to end. Water and sand streamed from his nose and ears and the crotch of his trunks. He wiped the snot away from his upper lip with the back of his forearm. When at last he was able to open his burning eyes, Sara was standing beside him. He read not only amusement but also sympathy in her smile. It was then that he started to love her.

She had left him twice and each time he had felt as though he could not live. He felt now that soon something was going to happen to pull them apart again. It has something to do with Tijuana and Sara feeling ugly, he thought. Thinking about how it had been between them, Paul knew it would never be that way again. He was resigned to it, and was glad that he did not feel any worse than he did.

Sara called. "It's windy outside."

"It was coming up when I was walking home." He could hear it through the window by the telephone.

"The wind made me think of you. Haven't you noticed, whenever it's windy I call you?"

"I guess I never noticed."

"Jimmy? I can't go out tonight."

"Why not?"

"I can't tell you over the phone. Could we go out tomorrow night instead?"

"I guess so. I don't know. I guess so." His testicles ached for her.

"I love you, Jimbo. I would go out with you if I could." She started to cry.

"Is it your stepfather?"

"Yes."

"All right. It's all right. Please don't cry. We can go out tomorrow."

"Oh, Jim."

"Can I see you tonight? I could come over."

"No, Jimbo, not tonight. It's pretty bad here now. He hit my mother again. I can't talk anymore, Jimbo. He's going to come in here soon. He told me not to use the telephone."

"Are you going to be all right? You could come over here for the night."

"I'd better not, Jimbo. I'll be all right. I have to go now," Sara said quickly. "Call me tomorrow?"

"I will."

Somewhere behind her, her stepfather was shouting.

"I'm glad I called, Jimmy," Sara whispered into the phone.

He was sullen, he could not explain why. Driving, he kept his eyes fixed on the freeway. He felt Sara watching him.

"Shit," she said.

Paul did not say anything.

"That's where Murphy lives." She pointed to some apartments off to the right. "He's engaged now. To an Italian girl. He calls her his wop broad."

"Why are you telling me this?"

"I though you might be interested. Aren't you?"

"No."

"I didn't think you would be."

After a while she asked, "Why did you keep calling me for so long when I was so mean to you? Wasn't your pride hurt?"

"Yes."

"Then why did you keep calling?"

"I loved you. And I was determined not to lose you."

"Do you still love me?"

"Yes. I love you now more than ever," Paul said, meaning it.

"Then why don't you tell me sometimes, darling? I'm only a girl. I need to hear it."

"I'll say it more often."

"Say it now."

"I love you."

"I love to hear you say it. I love your voice."

"I think we missed the turnoff."

"I thought so."

"Why didn't you say something?"

"I don't know. I thought you knew where you were go-ing. I didn't want to injure your masculine pride."

"Well, it's sure as hell injured now."

Sara laughed.

Paul moved into the right-hand lane.

"Let's not turn around," Sara said. They were stopped at the bottom of the off-ramp. Paul turned right and pulled off the road onto the shoulder. There was no traffic.

"I've never seen you so happy."

"How do you know how happy I am?"

"I can tell it in your voice when you laugh."

"If you would stop tickling me I wouldn't laugh."

"I'm not tickling you."

"Well, something is stabbing me in the side."

"You mean this?" He made it move.

"Yes. That."

"Feel my hip, Jimbo. See how it's different from yours? Isn't it wonderful?"

"I want you, Sara."

"I want you too, darling. But what if I gave myself to

you?"

Paul laughed. "Then I would take you."

"And then what? What if I got pregnant? You'd leave me, Jimbo."

"I don't know if I would or not."

"You would, Jimmy. I don't like to admit it to myself either, but I know you would."

"I could wear something."

"No, darling. When it happens I want it to be just you and me, not you, me and B.F. Goodrich."

"Kiss my belly again, Jimmy. I wore these panties with the crocodile on them just for you. I knew this would be the night you'd see them. Can you see the crocodile, Jimmy? It's green."

"Yes. I can see it."

"Don't do that, Jimmy. Please."

"Why not?"

"Just please don't do it."

"All right."

"Why do you have to have a Volkswagen? How can you do anything in a Volkswagen?"

"My hard luck."

"Is that supposed to be a pun?"

"I don't know. But it hurts."

"I thought you were happy, darling."

"I am. It's a good hurt."

"Tell me you love me."

"I love you. Very much."

"Is there anything I can do?"

"I don't know."

"Would you like me to do this?"

"Yes."

"Would you kiss my belly, darling? Like you did before?"

"Yes. Yes."

"I didn't know it was so big. Don't laugh. How was I supposed to know?"

"The other night, Jimmy, it was horrible without you. My stepfather came home drunk and my mother wasn't there again. He hit me again, Jimmy. He hadn't struck me in more that a year but he was so angry and I felt so sorry for him. I guess that's why he hit me; I told him I felt sorry for him. I injured his pride. But I hit him back this time, Jimmy. I doubled up my little fist and I hit him in the eye. He was so surprised. He just went to bed, he didn't say a word, he just stood there looking at me, he was so surprised, and then he went to bed. This morning he had a black eye. He looked so funny.

"After I went to bed my mother came home and I could hear them shouting at each other. Mikey sleeps like a log. He didn't hear a thing. But I could hear them fighting in their bedroom. I think he hit her, too. He called her a slut. He said we were both sluts, she and I. He called me a whore, Jimmy.

"Then it got quiet and after a while my mother came into my bedroom. She sat down on my bed and she was crying, Jimmy. She put her arms around me and we held each other. Like two babies."

"It's all right. It's all right," Paul said.

"It isn't all right, Jimmy. It isn't. We just held each other and rocked back and forth. She was crying and she started saying the Lord's Prayer and then she wanted me to say it with her and I almost couldn't do it, Jimmy, I almost couldn't remember it, but I listened to her saying it and then it came back. Oh God, Jimmy, do you know how long it's been since I've been to church? Not since before my father left us. Not since years before my father left. We kept repeating it, 'Our father who art in heaven, hallowed be thy name,' until we stopped crying. There just weren't any more tears, Jimmy."

"It's all right, it's all right."

"No, Jimmy darling, my darling, my love, it isn't all right. It isn't."

When they came to the apartments where Murphy lived, Sara said, "Murphy lives there," and they laughed. After a while Sara said, "Jimbo?" and he answered, "Yes?" and turned so she could see that he was smiling. He knew that she was testing him and he was glad that he could show her honestly that she did not have to worry about what he was feeling. Sara smiled too. "Nothing."

The house was dark when they pulled up.

"Park in the driveway. Sonny likes to park by the curb."

Paul turned off the engine.

"Would you like to come in?"

It sounded so strange, so formal, her asking this, as if she was prepared to deny what had happened between them, that Paul was put off. But then he saw that she was still afraid of him, afraid that he might say no, and was hiding behind the formality.

"Yes," he said.

"Sonny's coming. Turn on the light."

Sara's stepfather stood in the doorway.

"Where's your mother?"

"I don't know."

"I'm sick."

"The bathroom is through there."

They could hear him retching. Paul imagined him bent over the toilet bowl.

"He's drunk again. I didn't even have time to fix my bra. By boobs are down here."

"What are those?"

"My bra. I just pulled out the points. Here, hook me."

He had already forgotten how smooth her skin was. She turned. "Here." She took his hand and thrust it between her legs. "Oh."

Sonny had returned. He was leaning against the wall. Paul did not know what he had seen.

"Young fellow, I think it's time for you to leave."

"All right."

"Where's your mother?"

"I told you, I don't know."

"I want you out of here in three minutes, fellow. I'm going to bed," he said to Sara.

He went out of the room. From the back he looked even bigger than he did from the front.

"Do I have to go?"

"You'd better leave. He gets awfully mean when he's drunk, especially when my mother isn't here."

"Will you be all right tonight?"

"I'll be all right. He's too drunk to do anything tonight. I love to see him get sick. The bastard."

"Are you sure you'll be all right?"

"You'd better leave, Jimmy. He'll be checking on us in a minute."

"I'm afraid to leave you."

"Don't be afraid, darling. Will you kiss me goodnight? That's a good boy. Now leave."

Sonny came out of the bedroom in his bathrobe and sat down on the sofa. "I'm going to wait up for your mother." He fixed his eyes on the door.

He had already dozed off by the time Sara was finished in the bathroom, but walking through the hallway to her room she saw his head snap up and his eyes open. She could not tell if he saw her watching him. You never know what a drunk sees, she thought.

She wore a set of Mikey's pajamas. She would have liked to sleep nude tonight. It would be nice to look at herself in the mirror, then creep naked into bed between the cool sheets she had put on this morning, to feel their fresh scratch against her skin as she fell asleep. She enjoyed admiring her body in the mirror before going to bed. Her breasts were too small, she believed, but the rest of her was proportioned well and it gave her pleasure to run her hands over her hips and to feel her pubic hair springy and soft beneath her palm. She was "a fine piece," as the expression has it, she thought. She could bear children, she knew, if she had to.

But tonight she wore Mikey's pajamas. She did not know what Sonny might do in his stupor. It was true he had never bothered her, but she was afraid of him tonight. She hoped her mother would come home soon.

If she could not feel the sheets against her skin, at least she could hear them rustle as she moved between them. She listened for the wind but it had died down. Then she remembered that it was yesterday that the wind had blown so, and that today there had been nothing unusual in the weather except that the sky had been so blue in the morning before the smog settled in.

She thought about the wind and how she liked to walk in it, leaning into it when it blew against her. She liked its blowing her hair so that she felt it pulling on her scalp, she holding her books against her chest, flattening her breasts, aware of the difference in sensation between her breasts and her chest, and aware even of the difference in feeling between her nipples and her breasts, the nipples so sensitive they sometimes hurt and even bled once from chafing against her bra. She thought how she liked Jimbo to touch her breasts, and how he liked to play with them, and how the wind reminded her of him, she didn't know why, she could probably figure it out but she didn't want to because you lose the magic of a thing when you figure it out. I like him to suck on my titties, that part of herself she called her nighttime self thought, I asked him to kiss my belly please like he did before and he sucked on my titties again which was what I wanted him to do.

I like playing with him, only my hand touched it but it made him feel so good, I thought he was going to cry when I kissed it, I was afraid he would come in my mouth but I kissed it anyway. He frightened me when he put his hand between my legs, I knew if he kept on I wouldn't be able to

stop, I asked him please not to but I really wanted him to
but he stopped and played with the curls and then he came
all over my hand and I thought how strange it was that here
were billions of babies that would never be born and I felt
sad but awe-struck too, and I almost cried but I laughed instead and then we saw where some of his sperm had hit the
windshield and was dripping down in a slow milky blob and
we both of us laughed, it was so funny and sad but I don't
know if he thought it was sad.

I wish he had done it to me. I wanted him to. Murphy
did it to me. I don't want to think about that but I know I
will, I can't stop my thoughts. I don't like it with Murphy,
he makes me feel slimy but he makes me come, I can't come
with anybody else, I should say climax, it's a nicer word,
I have to respect myself and I won't unless I think well of
myself. I used to wish I was Marjorie Morningstar but now I
know it's just a book, Jimbo read it too, I didn't know he had
read it and I started saying things that I thought she would
say and he caught me at it but I denied it but I guess that
means that I still wish I was Marjorie Morningstar and could
be sure of the outcome of whatever happens to me. God, I
wish he would do it to me, I want him inside me, I wish he
would stop just playing with me, he gets me so hot he makes
me go back to Murphy, but I would go back to Murphy
anyway, there's no point in lying. I told Jimbo that I made
a rule, you can't go back to somebody you don't love, but I
called Murphy the same night, so I lied to both of us. I told
Jimmy that I was a quarter slut, I couldn't say it plainly and
he didn't understand, I wish he would understand, I'm afraid
if he did he'd leave me, then I said I was a two-bit whore and
he just looked at me like what was I talking about, he still

didn't understand, I was ready to cry it hurt so much, damnit, damn him, I am, I am crying....

Murphy's a bastard. He's going to marry an Italian girl, he calls her his wop broad but he doesn't say it affectionately. When I told him that Negro policeman in Hollywood had made me pregnant he wanted to marry me right away, it made me cry, I felt so sad, but maybe he didn't believe me, maybe he knew I was lying so he felt safe, it would be like him, he's a real bastard, and then after we would have made all the arrangements for the wedding and I would have had my dress and the flowers ordered he would have backed out, he could do it. Mother likes him, she says an older man is good for a young girl, she says she wishes she had had someone like him when she was my age. The first time he did it to me after he did it to me the first time he knew he could do whatever he wanted and it didn't matter what I said and at first he was laughing at me because he knew it didn't matter what I did or said and he got my panties off and then he was kissing me through my dress, my breasts and belly and my hips through my dress and my between my legs and my legs and my hole opened and there was nothing I could do or wanted to do and it ached so and it was so good I was crying and I came and came and came. And after a while he wanted to turn on the lamp and I was afraid and I shouted at him not to turn on the light and he was surprised, I could feel him being surprised in the dark, and he didn't turn on the light and after a while I let him take off my dress and I pulled him down on me and he pressed me, pressed against me, and I opened and it was like I was someone else and it didn't matter what had happened before.

Sometimes Sonny comes into my room. He frightens

me, he just stands there looking at me when he thinks I'm asleep, I can't tell what he's thinking. Sonny is a drunk, he says he's going to beat up Mikey as soon as Mikey is eighteen but the way Mikey is growing now and the way Sonny is dissipating maybe Mikey will beat him up if Sonny still has the courage to fight him then. I'd like to see Mikey beat him up but Sonny's awfully tough, he used to be a sergeant in the army, he's always saying how much he used to fight and how the men in his squad or company or whatever it was used to respect him because he was always willing to fight anybody who wanted to fight him. Sonny hit me once, he called me a whore, he said I was a whore like my mother. Mother keeps throwing him out, the house is in her name, it's left over from when Daddy was here, but he keeps coming back, once she even got a separation, she filed the separation papers and Sonny stayed away for almost six weeks, they went to bed as soon as he walked in the door, I had to go out in the yard, I was laughing so hard. Now she's pregnant so I guess Sonny is here for good.

When Daddy left it was Christmas and I tried to break all the colored balls that were hanging from the Christmas tree, I tried to squeeze them in my little hands until they broke, and I did too, I broke all of them except one, it was too strong, maybe I could do it now if I tried. Mother is a whore, everybody knows it, maybe that's why Sonny drinks so much, maybe that's why Daddy left, I wish I knew, but it doesn't matter now. I like to see Sonny get sick when he's drunk, he's a real s.o.b. The other night when we were lying on the sofa in the dark my bra was almost up to my neck, God, we were hot, we heard Sonny throwing up in the toilet, you could hear it splashing in the water, he walked right past us and didn't even see us, he didn't even know I was home, Mother wasn't home yet either.

When Jimbo said he wanted me I could feel his erection against my belly through his clothes and my clothes too, it was so hot and hard, I said what would you do if I gave myself to you. Take you, he said, and he laughed and it started to get soft, it was much more comfortable with him after he laughed and it got soft again but he always talks about finding those dead horses in the desert, I don't know why he dwells on them so, the animals had gotten to them, he said, carrion eaters, and there were twenty or thirty horses almost in a circle and they had been there for so long there was no longer any smell from them and even the flies and maggots had gone, he talks about them all the time, there was still flesh on the bodies, the carcasses, he said, but nothing was eating them anymore, he didn't know what had killed them, maybe somebody shot them, the eyes and all the guts were gone....

I told him about when I used to live in Whittier and La Habra and about the Mexicans who used to pick oranges and everybody was afraid of them when they went into town on Sunday, you couldn't see anybody else on the street, I used to watch out of the window, I wasn't afraid of them, it never occurred to me to be afraid of them, Mother didn't know I used to bring them cookies after lunch sometimes when I was a little girl, I was already starting to learn a little Spanish, they were so gentle and kind, everybody was afraid probably because they spoke Spanish not English and their skin was dark and their hair was black and they didn't smile at anyone but me and they smiled at me because I was gentle and kind too so he thinks about his dead horses and I think about La Habra and Whittier when I was just a little girl and orange trees were there instead of houses and people, and the Mexicans aren't there anymore, they're back in Mexico probably, I wonder if they ever think of me, I was just a little girl then, that's how they would remember me if they do, some of them probably have gray hair now but I can't picture it any more than they could imagine me as I am now. Jimbo says there is no tomorrow, everything is today, sometimes I am afraid for him, sometimes he seems so terrible inside himself, I don't like to think that everything is now and all of the things behind us are now or not at all and when we die nobody will care, I'd like to have his baby he was going to buy some rubbers but I said I wanted him inside me not him and me and B.F. Goodrich together, that was the night I let him take off my panties I knew he would I wore the black ones with the green crocodile on them he thought it was funny maybe he's a virgin it would be worse if he was a virgin, he told me he hoped I was never without a man he considers himself a man he's almost filled out I asked him why and he said he never wanted to have to think of me being alone I guess I love him but I wish some things were different I wish he would just go ahead and do it to me Murphy fucked me but I haven't been faithful to him he doesn't care he asked me how many guys I've done it with I told him six he didn't care it was just like it always is with Murphy once he grabbed my ankles and dropped me on my head the bastard.

Jimbo says his testicles ache when he talks to me on the telephone he turns off the lights so that it is like we don't have bodies, we are only our voices in the air together his testicles ache he says he has wet dreams when he thinks about me at night he comes in his sleep when I'm excited I can smell

myself men smell different when they're excited stronger but
not as strong as women all Mother cares about is what men
have in their pants once I heard her and Sonny laughing and
when I went to the bathroom her door was open and she
was on top of Sonny he has thick legs and she had it in her
mouth her head was going up and down up and down like
she had it up in her between her legs only she didn't she had
it in her mouth she cheats on Sonny even though he almost
always knows and beats her up sometimes Mother has flabby
legs the insides of her legs are flabbywrinkledsoft her breasts
sag she has big breasts but they're fat they puff out of her bra
she can only excite the men who come into the bar where
she works I could do it to myself tonight Murphy says that
sometimes when he's horny he fucks his hand I could do that
to myself and dream of somebody not Murphy, Bill lives
across the street I should return that book to him I'll never
read it now I've had it too long Bill and Peggy used to visit
us but Sonny didn't like them I don't think he ever said anything to them they just stopped coming over I'd like to talk
with Bill again sometime I could tell him about how Mother
and I prayed together after Sonny beat her up we said the
Lord's Prayer and Mother was crying and we held each other
like two little children lost in the dark and we said the Lord's
Prayer together but neither of us could remember how it
went we remembered most of it but we couldn't remember it
all and Mother began to cry again and I did too and we just
held on to each other I'm going to have to think of someone
if I'm going to do it with my fingers I could think about Bill
or Jimbo the others don't matter I never read *War and Peace*
I keep trying but it's so long and I forget who the people are
I wish I had been adopted by somebody when Daddy left I

used to dream that Bill and Peggy adopted me and I lived
happily ever after....

III

"I'm going for a swim."

Sara looked up at Paul, then down at her legs browning
on the sand.

"Go ahead. I won't stop you."

"I'll just drink," Dennis said. His features looked soft and
rubbery as though the muscles in his face had broken down.
Still, he may have been faking it.

Paul ran into the water until it was too deep to run.
He dived under the crest of a wave, came up in the trough
and swam out beyond the line of breakers. After a while he
turned on his back and let the swells roll under him.

It won't be long, he thought. Maybe next summer, maybe
even the end of this summer. He grimaced at the thought
of tourists discovering The Wedge. They probably have ex-
ploration parties out now. In his mind he saw them in their
Hawaiian shirts and Bermuda shorts, their legs like white
hickory spindles, men and women dressed identically, the
children miniatures of the adults.

Soon I'll have lost this beach, he thought, and a little
more of this ocean. California will be over by the time I'm
out of school. Well, there is always Mexico if you go south.
Paul turned on his stomach and swam. He caught a wave,
then a second one in to the beach.

"I was beginning to worry, you were in the water for so
long," Sara said.

"It's nice to know that you worry about me."

"Oh, shut up."

She lay back and closed her eyes against the sun. Paul followed the slow curve of her leg to the hidden mound with his eyes. He began to get aroused.

Sara stood up.

"I'm going down to the water."

He watched her brush the sand from the backs of her legs and walk over the rise of dry sand to the wet pack below.

Dennis put his empty in the trash bag and opened another.

"You were holding her hand while I was driving, weren't you?"

"We were holding each other's hand, yes," Dennis said.

"And when I went in for cigarettes you kissed her."

"I tried but she wouldn't let me." Dennis was staring at the line where water and sky met. He didn't look drunk now. "You have nothing to worry about."

"I'm sorry."

"You knew all along, didn't you?"

"I could see it."

"Didn't it bother you?"

"Sure."

"Why didn't you say something?"

"Would it have mattered?"

"It would have mattered to me. I felt so guilty the whole time."

"You should have stayed away from her then."

"The hell with it. I'm going for a walk. If you decide to leave, go on without me. I'll find a ride."

Dennis' figure diminished toward the water. When it approached Sara, it turned away as she began to speak.

Sara came up. Paul admired the flow of long muscle under the flesh of her thighs as she walked.

"Jimmy?"

"Yes?"

"He didn't mean anything. I mean, he was before you. Isn't that what counts? What matters is what happens from now on, right?"

"Yes. That's all that matters, really." Dennis was a stick figure down the beach. "Let's go now."

"What about Dennis? He'll be back soon."

"He can thumb a ride. Or catch a bus."

"You don't have to be cruel. It wasn't his fault."

"Come on."

"…All right." She began to pick up her things. "It's over now," she said, more to herself than to him. "There won't be anything more for us, will there?"

Paul didn't look at her.

"It really has nothing to do with Dennis, has it?"

"No."

"I didn't think so."

She started back through the sand to the car.

Driving home, they did not talk. Several times Sara turned as though to say something but each time the words did not come out.

Paul drove without thinking. Then he began to think and he did not like what he thought and he forced himself to stop. After a while he began to think again but it was still painful and he made himself think of other things.

When he saw the horses in the desert it was like seeing the world, they were just there in the sand and rock and the sagebrush around them, thirty of them, horses and mules, the eyes were gone and the guts and everywhere there had been soft flesh it was gone. They were lying on their sides in a circle on the slope of a hill, it was like when I saw that auto accident in front of our house, that guy lying on the lawn, his brains coming out, I couldn't turn away until a fly settled on the brown of his eye and I knew he was dead, and then I could walk away because I knew he wasn't looking at me.

When I was drunk that time I fell down in the street I couldn't get up Sara was at the party with somebody I don't remember who she let him feel her breasts she let him take off her bra she told me when they parked I was lying in the street and somebody said "Get up, the cops are here," and I got up somebody helped me across the street and there was a Mexican guy, Rudy, who lived there the cops came and they said, "Who's that, Rudy?" and Rudy said I was his brother they knew he was lying and the cops said, "Are you staying clean?" and Rudy said, "Yeah, he's my brother," and they went away and Rudy said they were stupid whites and I didn't say anything until I said, "But I'm white too," and Rudy said, "That's all right, man, you're okay, you're just a drunk kid. You better watch out, they'll be after you now, you better stay out of this town for a while. Now me, I get drunk sometimes and sometimes I shoot up but not so much anymore, but I always know where the cops are, like I knew that party was gonna get busted tonight, man, so they put me away once three years out of my life, man, so as far as they know, I'm clean, but I hate the white blue-eyed motherfuckers and they know it." I said, "Only Negroes aren't white, man." But Rudy said, "No, man, anybody who ain't one of them ain't white."

It was as though we were mirrors for each other, Paul thought, like in *Snow White*, seeing ourselves in the reflection of the other as we wished we could be.

"What?" Sara asked.

Paul did not realize he had said anything.

PART TWO

The Moral Life of Soldiers
The American Education of a People's Army Officer

THE MORAL LIFE OF SOLDIERS

I

As a child, I wanted to be a poet.

One summer during my adolescence, my parents arranged for me to go to Hue to study with a monk who was a poet. When the summer ended and I had to return home, my teacher told me he would visit me periodically so that I could continue my training, if less formally than in Hue. He came once to my parents' house, then never returned. Until shortly before my mother died, I did not know why the monk did not come again to guide and criticize my literary efforts.

When my mother was already very ill and knew that she was going to die soon, she told me that she had pulled my teacher aside the one time he came to our house and asked him to discourage me from pursuing a literary life. There was no money in it, my mother said.

"Was that why he did not come back, because you asked him not to?" I asked.

"No," my mother said. "He did not return because he could not bring himself to behave falsely toward you." He had seen that I was talented, and rather than deny my talent, he removed himself from my life.

I asked my mother why, if she had not wanted me to have a literary life, she had agreed to allow me to study with the monk for a summer. I knew that my father had wanted me to pursue poetry. As a younger man, before the obligations of family life consumed his time, he had written poetry and he had never lost his love for it, or his regret that he had not continued to write. I had overheard the lengthy discussion my parents had had concerning my study with the poet-monk. I had been impressed by my father's vehemence, as he usually deferred to my mother's wishes, and I had been surprised that my mother had given in.

"I did not know you had a talent," she said. She appeared to be in agony as she said this. At first I interpreted her pain as coming from the recognition that she had betrayed my ambitions and my trust in her, but in a moment I realized that it was the decay of her body that so tormented her. "If I had known you had a talent, I never would have agreed to your going to Hue."

She wanted me to make my career in my uncle's export business. Instead, I became a soldier. I served in two armies, one after the other. I say one after the other because I want to make clear that while I was with each, I was loyal to it; I did not serve in one in order to spy on it for the other. While the peoples of both the United States and Viet Nam may choose to regard me with suspicion, as indeed some of those who know of my career do, I want to assure them that my loyalty has always been with them, one after the other.

My life has been filled with the stuff of legend and adventure, but it has also been a difficult one. While I rose to receive many honors and responsibilities, my body suffered much in the service of my government and my country. I was wounded many times and left for dead or as irretrievable on two occasions.

Often I have listened to young people exalt some of those incidents of war which, at the time I experienced them, meant only toil, misery, and death. I admit that I have been disconcerted to find myself vilified by others, particularly Americans, for allegedly having perpetrated almost unimaginable barbarities. I say "almost" unimaginable because I have come to believe that whatever cruelty may be imagined as inflicted upon a human being, this horror has indeed been committed against someone, even against entire populations. I am a child, after all, of the twentieth century. But I was not one of the perpetrators.

What attracted me to the soldier's life, and what held me to it, was neither the romance, of which I have seen none, nor the opportunity for sadism, the practice of which did not appeal to me. (I will say that, as a young officer, I did my utmost to prosecute those who committed the most egregious acts of barbarism, and as a senior commander, I punished any act of cruelty, no matter whether prompted by sadistic impulse or by revenge against the enemy for his own cruel acts.) No, what impelled me, if you have not already surmised it, was my personal revolt against the authority of my parents, especially my mother's. But what sustained me was my fascination with the moral life of the soldier. For most of my life, I have been interested in the question of why a soldier will choose one path to follow over any other.

Every facet of a soldier's life is filled with moral ambiguity, even those that, at first glance, seem to indicate clearly what one's stance or course of action should be. I offer as examples two stories. The first is of an incident that occurred during the American war in Viet Nam. It was told to me by an American lieutenant I met in a transit camp where I had gone to observe the interrogation of American prisoners. I will relate it to you as he related it to me.

His platoon was about to go into a village when the lieutenant joined it. He had been in the country for five days, enough time only to receive his briefings in the city before being sent to the countryside. That afternoon his platoon captured one of our soldiers. When they set up their night camp, the lieutenant radioed his commander for a helicopter to evacuate the prisoner.

It will be dark soon, the commander said. He doubted that a pilot would be willing to fly at night to pick up a prisoner.

The lieutenant said his situation was too insecure to keep the prisoner with him.

The commander agreed with the lieutenant's assessment.

"Well, what should I do, sir?"

The commander did not reply.

"What do you want me to do, sir?"

Again there was no reply. The lieutenant felt emptiness engulf him, drawing something out of him so that he felt the emptiness inside himself as well as without.

He set down the radio. He was crying. He walked over to where the prisoner lay tied up and aimed his rifle at him. He caught his breath and pressed the trigger. The rifle did not fire and he realized he had forgotten to release its safety. But he heard then from left and right the shrill, ear-piercing clap of his platoon's M-16s discharging in unison.

The lieutenant knew suddenly that in causing him to forget to release his safety, and in moving his platoon up beside him and having them fire the killing shots, Jesus Christ had performed a miracle on his behalf, for the prisoner was dead and the lieutenant was blameless. It was upon this realization that the lieutenant accepted Jesus Christ as his god and savior.

In moral ambiguity lies freedom—for the individual, if not for the collective. The lieutenant was not strong enough to accept this freedom, or at least the responsibility that accompanies it, or perhaps he was paralyzed by the prospect of freedom and responsibility. This self-concern of so many American officers, and the expectation that enlisted soldiers would be loyal to them—is it any wonder that American soldiers sometimes killed their officers? But when I was the age the lieutenant was when faced with his dilemma, I did not have the strength to accept freedom either.

The second story: I was a student at an American officer-training course at a base in Georgia not long after the second war on the peninsula ended, when, in spite of all of our effort and our expenditures in blood and materiel, we had been defeated and we believed it was simply a matter of time before our enemy exploited this fact. (I note that what I mean here by "our" and "we" is the south of Viet Nam during this time; I realize that the notion of the transfer of loyalties may be confusing for Western readers.)

During an exercise called "Company in the Assault," a fellow student was killed. We were positioned at the base of a hill when the command came to move forward. The man who died probably jammed the butt of his rifle into the ground to aid in getting to his feet; we had been warned by our instructors to avoid doing just that. The weapon discharged, the bullet entered the underside of the man's mouth and came out the top of his head, penetrating his helmet and flying off into space. That is probably what happened.

But the ballistics laboratory, or so we students were informed by the investigators from the Criminal Investigation Division, determined that the man had been shot with an M16, which fired a .22 caliber round, while he and everyone else on the range had been armed with M14s, which fired a 7.62 millimeter bullet. So on a Saturday morning shortly after the death of the student, thirty-three investigators in civilian clothes ensconced themselves at thirty-three tables in the battalion's mess hall and began the interrogation of the company by calling in the first thirty-three men in line at the door.

Much of the procedure was silly. The investigators were obviously under orders to interview the entire company, regardless of each man's proximity to the student when he was shot. I, for instance, was in a different platoon, located one hundred meters from the dead student's, and did not have a clear line of sight to the dead man.

Once this was established, the investigator, a soft-voiced young man with hair the color of which makes you think of lion cubs, placed his pen down and asked if I had noticed the student who was leaving the table as I arrived. I had. The investigator asked if I knew him. No, although I had seen him in the company compound a number of times. The investigator said that this student had been beside the man who was killed when the incident occurred. The student had told the investigator that the man had struck the ground with his rifle butt when they received the order to move out, and that the rifle had discharged as the man was standing up.

I asked how this could explain the man's having been shot with an M16.

The investigator shrugged as though that theory held no interest for him. He said the student had told him that he had seen the bullet, as if in slow motion, leave the muzzle of the man's rifle and enter his head. The investigator asked me if I thought it was possible to see a bullet as the student said he had seen it. I displayed the palms of my hands as though to dispel any suggestion that I might be concealing something. "Anything is possible," I said, and I laughed as if to say, "But not this." But I did not say it. And by not saying it, I knew that I was allowing the investigator to make of my laughter what he wished.

That is what has stayed with me: my own laughter upon recognizing that a fantasy was masquerading as reality. And more: my complicity in pretending that the fantastic was not fantastic, that it might be true and even reasonable. Who knew what actually had happened? Not the technicians in the ballistics laboratory with their fantasies of murder, not the witness who claimed to have seen what cannot be seen, not the investigators, and not I. Eventually the investigation was dropped.

Although the death of the student, with the ensuing investigation, was a minor affair compared with some of the situations I would encounter later, it was a watershed event in my life, for until this time I had not regarded myself as malleable as were other people, as a part of the horde, so to speak. I had seen myself as a distinct human being, and I had looked at others as individuals as well. The uniformity demanded by the army, by any army—indeed, by any country, apart from its army—was only a veneer, or so I had thought.

But I knew, after this incident, that I could be anything, that I could be made into anything, and that I had little to say about it.

It occurs to me only now, as I write this memoir, that my laughter was a message to myself, telling me that I, too, had become an accomplice.

II

Soon after I graduated from officers' training and was commissioned a lieutenant in the Army of the Republic of Vietnam, I was given the opportunity to attend several advanced schools. As the economic and psychological depression that had begun to assail my country boded little good for its soldiers, and particularly as my own army encouraged me to acquire whatever further training was available, I submitted my application to several schools. Barely a soldier myself, I still had the sense to avoid, if I could, the many of my countrymen who desired to cripple our country's military and punish its individual soldiers for having lost the last war.

In those years, the American schools were considered very good—if not as good as the British, better than those offered by the French. I attended a number of elite infantry schools, including the one I mentioned in the first chapter, parachute school, Ranger school, and a Special Forces course. I even went through a high-altitude parachute course, though I never afterward found a use for this particular training.

After completion of the Special Forces course, as part of an officer exchange program between the United States and my own country, I was invited to serve with an American

Special Forces group in Central America. I was a special
staff officer of the group for more than a year. My position
was called "special" because I reported directly to the commander rather than to one of the coordinating staff. What
this meant was that I had no specific role and no authority.
I did not resent this. I understood that, before anything else,
I was a foreigner to the Americans, who are not less xeno-
phobic than my own people, and although I was a graduate
of a number of their elite schools, I was still only an adjunct
to their army.

Most of these officers, unlike many in the American army
at that time, took themselves and their work very seriously.
This was during one of those periods between major wars,
and while most army units permitted their officers minimal
duty and maximum leisure, the Special Forces group extracted maximum duty, allowing little time for leisure. It was one
of those organizations the American sociologist Lewis Coser
called "greedy institutions." But it was greedy for a reason. If
the rest of the army was standing down, this group was not.
It was inserting assassination teams into Venezuela, rescue
teams into Colombia, combat teams into Guatemala and
Peru. It provided bodyguards to the president of Bolivia and
instructors in the arts of interrogation to the Argentineans.

I will say now that I know of these activities by the Americans only from the stories the soldiers told after returning
from tours of duty in other countries. They told these stories,
which I believe are true although undoubtedly embellished,
because they so often despised themselves for what they had
done or permitted to be done, and sought out people such as
myself, outsiders, who were willing to listen to them without
comment. Insulated as I was from these activities, hearing

only the occasional vignette which, to my youthful ears, recalled the romance of the tales of ancient times—guns instead of swords and arrows, of course, stealth and wit, the
hunter and the hunted, suffering redeemed—rather than
events in a vast epic of terror and subterfuge, I pushed them
out of my mind as the product of guilty consciences of a
handful of soldiers. They did not fit into the folklore that
had been part of my informal education, the stories my father told me when I was small, at night before I fell asleep.
(I wonder now what stories fathers who are veterans of our
wars tell their children.) It was many years before I could recall them from the mental compartment where I had stored
them. When I remembered them, and the soldiers who had
told them to me, it was almost as though I was hearing them
for the first time.

When revolutionaries murdered the Bolivian dictator, his
American bodyguards, all of whom escaped the ambush, ap-
plauded his death. So I was told. When a combat team returned from what was called a "hot mission" in Guatemala,
one of the noncommissioned officers on that team wrote a
letter to his representative in the American Congress, asking
how it was in their nation's interest to order its soldiers to
do some of the things they had done. All of this occurred in
an era when journalists made love with government officials
and the American mass media turned brutality into patri-
otic sentimentality. That is to say, nothing resulted from the
sergeant's letter except that he was not sent out on a mission
again for the remainder of his tour in Latin America. I heard
of him again on the peninsula where he led a reconnaissance
team. A month later he disappeared in the Cambodian forest with most of his team and was not seen again, at least by

the Americans. I remember him very well. His name was
Bott.

III

In Panama, where I spent nearly all of my sixteen months
with the Special Forces, I enjoyed myself very much.

The women of Panama! How I loved them! They came
from everywhere, from Medellín, from Lima, from La Paz,
and from as far north as Canada. Some were controlled by a
syndicate and spent only three months in a city before they
were removed to another city. The syndicate did not want
them to grow stale, nor to grow too fond of a lover, so it kept
moving them. Even this I found fascinating—the power to
mobilize people for one's own ends. Think of it! Think of
the calculations necessary to relocate even a single battalion
of prostitutes.

Other women were local. They came from villages into
the city to earn their living and to enjoy the high life. I met
one woman whose English was perfect, though her accent
pinched my ears. I had bought a skewer of roast meat from
a sidewalk vendor and had taken it up the street away from
the noise of the saloons. I had just finished eating it when a
light-skinned woman said in clear English: "Why don't you
go upstairs?" She had red hair and wide hips and was smiling. "Don't you want to dance?"

I turned around. The light over a doorway revealed a sign
in faded blue and red paint advertising a dance hall. I turned
back to the woman. "I don't know how to dance."

"That's too bad. Would you like a blow job?"

The transition, or lack of transition, from an act of socially acceptable movement to one of coarsest intimacy made me laugh. I let her take my hand. She led me to the end of the block, then into a maze of alleyways. "Don't be afraid," she said. In fact, I had begun to suspect that she was guiding me to a colleague who would beat me up, perhaps even kill me, for the little money I carried.

We came on some children playing hopscotch, or something like it, in the spilled light of the ramshackle houses. One of them said: "Leave the *chino* alone." Another said: "Don't bring the *chino* here." And another: "You always bring the *gringos* here. We don't like them or you." I had been in Panama for several months by this time and my Spanish, though still rudimentary, was good enough for me to understand these comments. One of the children threw something small at us. I heard it bounce off a wall.

"Don't worry, they won't do anything." She firmed her grip on my hand, perhaps to inhibit me from running away as well as to reassure me. "Did you understand them?"

"Yes."

"Your Spanish is good."

"So is your English. Where did you learn it?"

"In the States."

"When were you in the States?"

"Ten years ago. I lived in New York for two years. I was married to a *yanqui*. This is my house."

We went into a small construction made of unpainted planks. When she turned on the light I saw that there was only one room. She had tacked photographs of North American film stars on the walls. The photographs had been cut out of magazines.

"Why don't you take your clothes off?"

I pulled my shirt off over my head. There was no place to sit but on the bed. I slipped off my shoes, then my trousers.

"You have a nice body."

She undressed. Her breasts were heavier than I had guessed they would be. I had not expected her to excite me so.

"You like my body," she said.

"Yes."

"Do you want me to leave the light on?"

"Yes."

"Lie back."

As she worked over me, I stroked her cleft. I liked giving her pleasure as she gave me pleasure. I felt a union with her. Then she did something I had not had done to me before and I gasped.

"Do you like that?"

"Oh, yes."

She did it again. My reaction was the same. I gave myself up to her and thrust violently against her until I climaxed.

She got a cloth off a shelf and wiped her breast. Then she dampened the cloth in a basin and wiped my groin with it. Afterward, she sat down beside me.

"How much do I owe you?" I asked.

She did not answer, but asked, "Do you want to have a party?"

"A party?"

"I'll get my girlfriend and we'll have a party. She's very pretty. I'll tell her to bring some vodka."

I was silent. I brushed her left nipple with my thumb. I felt suddenly very sad.

"You can fuck me dog style."

I swung my legs over the side of the bed. "I don't think so."

"All right."

She handed me my trousers.

"Why do you want me to stay?"

"You're nice. You didn't beat me."

"Do men often beat you?"

She nodded. "You're my first man tonight. Maybe you'll be lucky for me."

I took some money from my wallet.

"Is this enough?"

"Only ten more and you could have a party. I'll pay for the vodka."

"No. Thank you."

And so I left. I saw her again on the street perhaps a month later, but she seemed not to remember me. What strikes me now, what has remained with me so many lifetimes since, was her loneliness. I think about her and wonder if she is even alive. How quickly everything changes. How short are our lives. Yet that loneliness endures, as if it were a contagion that travels from one person to another simply by the latter's acknowledging it. And the sadness I began to feel at my first perception of it remains.

IV

Although I was a commissioned officer, I was, as I indicated, not truly accepted by the American officers. Perhaps because of this rejection, I was adopted by the noncommissioned officers as, if not exactly one of their own, certainly something more than a mascot. Many evenings when I did not have the money to spend in Colón, or when I was too tired from the day's events to make the journey, I dressed in mufti and joined my NCO friends at their club.

On one occasion, somebody brought in a number of women from Colón. One of my friends, Sergeant Worden, wanted nothing to do with them, as he was angry with women, believing that everybody was laughing at him behind his back for his having been cuckolded by his lover. It had happened in Lima when his lover fellated Sergeant Rivera. Sergeant Rivera said he had only been trying to show Sergeant Worden that a woman's nature does not change simply because she has fallen in love. Sergeant Rivera said he had been trying to inform Sergeant Worden, as the old owe it to the young to educate them. Sergeant Worden's lover was reportedly unhappy that Sergeant Worden no longer loved her; she had done what she had only to earn her living.

Music came from the jukebox. A senior NCO named Moscowicz asked one of the women to dance. When she was in his arms, he asked, "What's your fuckin' *llama*, baby?"

This was very funny. Like many of the Americans, Sergeant Moscowicz had not attempted to learn more than the most vulgar, most fundamental Spanish, what it was absolutely necessary to know in order to satisfy his appetites. Aside from using that single word of Spanish ungrammatically, he had displayed his boorishness even in his use of English. This was the funniest part, and not only I but also the Americans I sat with laughed in delight.

The woman, understandably confused, answered, "Qué?"

"Fuck it," Sergeant Moscowicz said as he twirled her to the music of a popular North American song.

A sergeant named Axelrod stood up on a barstool and
shouted for silence that did not come. He stamped his foot
on the stool. When he raised his foot a second time, Sergeant Worden, acting out of the meanness from which he
viewed the world, jerked the stool out from under him and
Sergeant Axelrod fell onto the bar where he was pinned by
a gigantic man, Specialist MacIvey, formerly a player with a
North American football team.

"Aircraft carrier!" Specialist MacIvey shouted, pulling
Sergeant Axelrod by his foot to the end of the bar and forcing other soldiers to vacate their seats in order to make room
for them.

"Aircraft carrier!" Specialist MacIvey shouted again. Men
poured their beer on the bar while others grabbed Sergeant
Axelrod's arms and legs.

"Landing!"

The men holding Sergeant Axelrod swung him belly-
down onto the bar where his forward momentum carried
him to the far end and out onto the floor where he lay without moving.

"Is he alive?" shouted Specialist MacIvey.

"He's alive!" shouted another soldier, having taken Sergeant Axelrod's pulse. "I'm a medic and I declare him alive!"

"Yea-a-a!" Specialist MacIvey screamed. Then, pounding
the bar with his fist, he yelled, "Barkeep! Food and drink for
my men!"

This episode was diverting, but not diverting enough to
keep my attention from Sergeant Moscowicz who was still
on the dance floor with his partner. As I watched, he slipped
his hand under her skirt and grasped her left buttock. She
pulled away and slapped him across his face. He slapped her

in turn. Each slapped the other once more. Then she left the floor.

Sergeant Moscowicz was sauntering toward the bar, his face red with the imprint of her fingers but smiling nonetheless, when she approached. She slapped him again, this time leaving a thin red line across his cheek from which blood immediately began to bead. It was only a moment before he realized what she had done. He took two steps back and one step forward and kicked her in the stomach. She doubled over and fell backward onto the floor, the razor blade making a tiny metallic sound as it also hit the floor. Other soldiers positioned themselves between Sergeant Moscowicz and his dance partner to prevent his doing her further harm.

Specialist MacIvey came to our table. "Goddamn!" he said. "Lieutenant, I want you to have a good time. You're not having a good time, sitting here by yourself. Okay, I know you're not by yourself, you're sitting with these other soldiers, but they're faggots, Lieutenant."

Two of my table mates started to stand up, but Specialist MacIvey said, "All right, I know you're not faggots. None of us are. Hell, I'm a faggot too. We all are. The point is, Lieutenant, you're not having a good time. Listen, you see that broad over there lying on the floor over there by that puddle of blood and vomit over there? Do you see her? I want you to go over there and pick her up and dance with her. Will you do that for me? Will you goddamn please go over there and dance with her and enjoy yourself? Life is short, Lieutenant! Of course, you are too. No, no, erase that, erase that!"

I was enjoying myself, although Specialist MacIvey did not see this. Perhaps "enjoying" is not the correct word. I was interested in an exchange between two NCOs who had seated themselves at the bar following Sergeant Axelrod's taxi down its length. One was a legend in the Special Forces: a captain in the infantry in the last great European war, a major in a parachute regiment during the war in Korea, he was now a master sergeant racing whiskey against retirement. The other, Sergeant Donaldson, was a younger man who had sat down beside the master sergeant while waiting for the barman to detach himself from a couple of drinkers at the far end of the bar.

"How old are you?" the older man, Sergeant Wain, asked the younger.

"What's the difference?"

"Answer me, goddamnit, or I'll put my fuckin' foot in your face."

"I'm twenty-two."

"Twenty-two. A baby. Still in your diapers." Sergeant Wain inhaled deeply and let his breath out slowly. "We don't like you. But we need you. Do you understand? We don't like you, but we need you. The army doesn't like you, but it needs you. Young blood. Young meat. There ain't enough of us left to fight the next war. So the army needs you. But we don't like you. Young meat. How old are you?"

"Twenty-two."

"Twenty-two. Too young for the last one. You ever hold a man's heart in your hand?"

"I don't understand."

"You wouldn't. You haven't been there yet. I reached back to grab my radioman to call for mortar fire and got a handful of his heart. He didn't know it. It was too late for him to know anything. Too fuckin' late."

Sergeant Donaldson held up three fingers to the barman.

"Get me one too."

Sergeant Donaldson held up four fingers.

"They decorated me for that action. I didn't want their fuckin' medal. I threw it away. Threw it. Away."

At a table beside mine, a stocky NCO, Sergeant Quintera, rose from his chair and went over to retrieve Sergeant Donaldson and three of the beers. They returned to a third soldier who had remained at the table, another young man, though older than Sergeant Donaldson. I had seen this sergeant in Colón a number of times and knew his name was Sergeant Hibbard.

"Pappy give you a hard time?" Sergeant Quintera asked.

"Something like that," Sergeant Donaldson said.

"He's all right when he's sober."

"He's not sober now."

"Pappy and I go back a long way. I knew him in Korea. I got Korea on the brain today."

"Tell him what the shrink said," said Sergeant Hibbard.

"Psychiatrist, man. He's a psychiatrist. I guess that's the same thing as a shrink, huh?"

"What did you see a shrink for?" Sergeant Donaldson asked.

"I'm telling you, man. Give me a chance. He wanted to know if I still have nightmares about the war. The Korean War. See, when I got back from Korea, they gave us forms to fill out. There was a question that asked if you ever had nightmares. I said I did. I guess somebody finally got around to reading them. I forgot all about them. I told the psychiatrist, it's been eleven years, man, I don't want to think about it. So I've got to go in for treatments once a week."

"What!"

"Once a week. Every week. Until he says I don't have to. He says I'll come in every week for an hour and we'll talk about my nightmares."

"Do you remember them?"

"Oh, yeah. They don't ever go away. I mean they're not nightmares anymore, but you still remember them from when they were. You'll find out, man. When you going over? You got your orders?"

"They haven't come in yet," Sergeant Donaldson said.

"Yeah. I don't have nightmares about Laos. Just Korea. I mean I don't have nightmares about Korea, but those are the only ones I remember. If I have them about Laos, I don't remember them. You know what I mean."

"Yeah. Strange."

"Strange all right. Did I ever tell you how it was at Chipyong-ni. You know Chipyong-ni?"

"I've heard of it."

"You have, huh? Pappy was there. So was I. What did you hear about it?"

"I don't remember."

"Uh-huh. I thought so. I'll tell you about it sometime. Not tonight. I don't want to think about it tonight."

"Fine."

"Fine, huh? What's fine? Why don't you guys get your asses out of here. I don't want to look at you. Fine. Get your asses out of here. That's it. Go."

This, I believe, was my first experience, albeit from a distance, with fear so violent that it produces a brutality hungering for annihilation. Yes, this is what I saw and heard issue from Sergeants Wain and Quintera: fear and the desire for death, to give it and to receive it. I did not understand then that the experience of war implants itself so corrosively in the mind of the soldier, its tendrils insinuating themselves into all aspects of its victim's personality, as never to release him. War, even in small doses, sentences both its participants and its observers to imprisonment for life. I understand this now, though I did not then, on that night in Panama: war eventually destroys everyone who comes near it. (Writing this paragraph, I begin to see that my purpose in composing this memoir is not, or at least not only, to explore the moral life of soldiers.)

But there were the women, always the women. And if I had begun to perceive the tragedy immanent in the experience of being human, I could still bury myself in the perfume of a women's arousal, smother myself in her flesh. I loved the details of women, the shape of their fingers, the way the nipple of one breast swelled more quickly than the nipple of the other, how one woman moistened so much sooner than another, the varieties of scent the body of a single woman emitted. Oh glory! Glory! In that time of my youth, a woman's sadness touched me, but I did not understand it as inherent in the female sex, at least the female sex as I have known it. And I did not know that it would engender such sorrow in me.

V

An opportunity arose to reside in a village on the Atlantic coast for a short time. The Americans had constructed an infirmary in this village and were training young, indigenous men and women to be nurses. In addition to the American medics who operated the infirmary, there were radiomen and an audio-visual team who occasionally showed old Disney cartoons or propaganda films idealizing U.S. activities in South and Central America.

We went by LCM from a small fort near the canal to the village of San Felipe. (I am sorry, but I do not remember from which base we embarked. It may have been Fort Sherman, but I recall the name of another small post, Fort Davis, that was nearby and which may have been where we put out from.) I say "we" because, to my surprise, I met on board Sergeant Donaldson whom I had last seen talking with his friends, Sergeant Hibbard and Sergeant Quintera, at the NCO Club. I noticed him before we cast off. A collection of four or five Panamanians was loading something on board—building materials, I think, cement powder or stucco, packaged in large, heavy paper bags. We soldiers and sailors watched them for several minutes and then—not on impulse, but as though he had been struggling against himself and finally had determined to go ahead with his original idea; I surmised this from the way in which his body seemed to propel itself forward, then withdrew, moved forward, then backed away again from the Panamanians—Sergeant Donaldson thrust himself into their midst and began carrying the bags onto the boat, shoulder to shoulder with the Panamanian stevedores. It was an obvious attempt to build solidarity, but solidarity with whom? With workers? With nationals from another country? Was he trying to break down the barriers of nationalism? To construct an alliance between North Americans and Panamanians? If the last, then against whom? The Cubans? No matter: by the time the bags were stacked neatly on deck, both he and the Panamanians were coated in the sheen of a drenching sweat and were slapping one another on the back and clasping hands in mutual congratulation.

Halfway to San Felipe the boat slowed, then stopped, and a crewman let out the anchor. In a few minutes most of the crew had strapped SCUBA tanks onto their backs and stepped off the lowered ramp into the water. I was not a diver, so I only observed these young Americans at play. Perhaps Sergeant Donaldson was not a diver either, for he also stayed on board.

We peered together over the edge of the ramp at the others in the water. We were able to see many fathoms down; I have no idea how many, but we watched the divers become small and then disappear into the darkness. The sun was very bright and the only clouds in the sky hung like cotton over the mountains to the south.

After twenty or thirty minutes, one diver and then the others made their way up out of the depths, slowly growing in size from small, colorful mammals to larger beings of the same species as myself. One by one, they bobbed to the surface. The last one out of the water had speared a small shark that had a yellow cast in its gray skin. It was still alive when they took it on board and the captain got a club he apparently kept for such a purpose and beat the shark on the head until it was dead. He took a knife and opened its bowels and, with his hands, extracted its guts and threw them into the water. To attract others, he said. One of the divers sliced a chunk of meat from the dead shark, put a hook into it and dropped it into the water. But, although we could see other sharks, brother to this one in size and coloring, they did not close on the bait their sibling had provided.

Sergeant Donaldson, still looking over the side of the ramp into the clear water, said, "Aren't they beautiful?"

The captain, who had come up behind us without my hearing him, said, "They're beautiful animals."

"They move so effortlessly. From here they seem as insubstantial as phantoms."

"But not from down there. Below, they're pure death."

"That's part of what makes them so beautiful. Knowing that they're true killers."

"It's getting too deep for me," the captain said. "So to speak." He returned to the bridge.

Sergeant Donaldson said, "It's like looking into eternity."

I peeked over the edge. I saw something dark and sinuous and shimmering cut through the blue water and pass under the boat. I drew back, afraid. The thing I had seen dwelt in the realm of death, and now it was beneath our feet. Sergeant Donaldson continued to stare into eternity, entranced. I moved away, to the center of the boat, and sat down. I brought my knees up to my chest and wrapped my arms around them and clasped my hands.

The boat started again. We had not gotten far past Portobello when we saw flying fish, their fins like veined wings, vibrating with such speed that they appeared as translucent as hummingbirds' wings. "They have some of the qualities of birds, but they are not birds," Sergeant Donaldson said. I did not respond. In any case, he seemed to be talking to himself rather than to me, as though he were trying to memorize something, perhaps a line from a poem, or a poem to be.

As we approached the reef at San Felipe, Sergeant Donaldson said, "It will be like this: the landing ramp will lower and we'll jump off into the water. The water will be about knee deep. It will be clear and blue and warm and we'll be able to see our boots magnified against the white sand. There will be sea urchins everywhere, both the black and the brown varieties. On the beach will be kids and a few adults and the kids will run to the village to announce our arrival. That is how it was when I was here before."

And that is how it was this time, with one difference: even before reaching dry sand, we saw a girl—Elena, I learned later—walking along the beach toward the village. She was looking over her shoulder with an affected coyness that I thought she must have learned from a North American film. When Sergeant Donaldson waved, she did not stop but continued toward the village as though she had not seen him. And behind her and behind the village was the forest, turning a deeper, blacker green as it led into the interior. And beyond the cypress and mangrove of swamp and low jungle were the mountains enswathed in the mahogany, pine and ironwood of higher jungle, and over and beyond the mountains were the big, thick-muscled, purple-bellied clouds that signaled heavy rain. I could see now what brought Sergeant Donaldson's thoughts to eternity and the natural order: he was in love with this country that was not his own, and this peasant girl who was as unlike him as... as... I was.

Sergeant Donaldson ran ahead and caught up to her on the point of land where the river meets the sea. I could see her pressed against him, mouthing words to him. He told me later that she said she loved him and that she had not believed them when the children told her that he had come back, not even when she saw him standing in the boat, but now that she could touch him she believed he had returned. When he told me all of this, he told me also that he wanted to spend his life in San Felipe.

The village lies a few meters from where the San Felipe River, after a four-day journey from the mountains, joins the sea. It is—or was then; I shall describe it as I knew it, though I am certain it has changed—a village of one dirt street and a number of pathways leading to plank houses edging the jungle. One could travel to the village by LCM, as we had, or on a small commercial vessel that serviced the village weekly, picking up fish and copra for its return to Colón. Or one could fly in by helicopter; the Americans had cleared an area near the river for use as a landing pad. Or one could walk to San Felipe along the coast or from the mountains, or paddle by dugout canoe down the river from the mountains. But no road led there, and there were no automobiles, so when I noted a street, as I did a moment ago, I meant, rather, an avenue that served to center the life of the village. Here two small general goods stores and a hotel were established, as well as a schoolhouse, the infirmary the Americans had built, and a number of gray, unpainted, wooden houses. Here was a small plaza where the national flag was raised on public occasions.

I shared a house with another officer, also a lieutenant, across the street from the infirmary. I no longer remember his name but I am certain he had the same surname as one of the early American presidents, Washington or Jefferson or Jackson, so let me call him Washington. Lieutenant Washington spent little time in the house except to entertain, so, save for one or two evenings a week, I had it to myself. The house beside mine, nearer the river, was occupied by Sergeant Donaldson and another NCO, Sergeant Lawrence, a tall young man with a pleasant disposition who seldom spoke. The two sergeants were the radio operators. The medics who managed the infirmary lived in a small room inside that building. The same boat that brought Sergeant Donaldson and me to San Felipe took back the two-man audio-visual team that had been there. They were not replaced, though they had left their equipment behind. It fell to Lieutenant Washington to show the cartoons and propaganda films, should he find an occasion to do so. The six of us then, two officers, two medics and two radio operators, composed the American presence, for, to the people of San Felipe, I was also an American.

I followed Sergeant Donaldson and the girl, Elena, to the village, keeping myself as inconspicuous as I was able, yet dogging their heels out of fear that I would lose my way amid the coconut palms and thick undergrowth that separated the village from the beach. They could not keep their bodies from colliding, their hands from clasping, their mouths from drinking each other, as if love could be expressed only by devouring its object. Yet, when the village was upon them, they pulled apart and proceeded as though they were the most chaste of acquaintances who happened by purest coincidence to meet each other as each was on his or her personal errand en route to this village.

Sergeant Donaldson indicated the house where I could find Lieutenant Washington. The lieutenant was not there and I dropped my duffel bag on a bare cot that I assumed had been set up for me. Looking out the window, I saw Sergeant Donaldson on the steps of the infirmary. A toothless woman was frantically pawing him. Villagers were crowding around. Sergeant Donaldson took something out of his bag and handed it to the woman. From my window, I took it to be a small bottle of perfume. People screamed with laughter. Although his back was to me, I could see Sergeant Donaldson's ears redden as though scalded. She kissed him firmly on the mouth and then went off with a man who had been standing beside her, apparently her husband.

I walked across the street in time to see Sergeant Donaldson give Elena a similar bottle of perfume. She accepted it silently—the people standing about were also silent—and took it to her house. For a young boy—his houseboy, I would later learn—he had brought a cloth belt and a brass military buckle. The boy, whose name was Abrilio, also accepted this gift without demonstration. To another boy, older, larger, he gave a clasp knife. This boy grinned happily as he took the knife. A box of bullets and tin of gun oil went to the local Guardia corporal who laughed hugely as Sergeant Donaldson gave him the oil.

Sergeant Donaldson asked about two men he called "the hunters." Someone said they were in the mountains. "I have something for them, too," Sergeant Donaldson said. Someone, a woman, said they would return tomorrow, or, if not tomorrow, then the day after. "Then I'll give it to them when they return," he said.

The gift giving over, Sergeant Donaldson walked across the street to the house he shared with Sergeant Lawrence. Of all of those who had waited to see what Sergeant Donaldson had brought to give away, few benefited by their patience.

Perhaps a week later, Sergeant Donaldson told me that the boy to whom he had given the clasp knife, Jaime, had once boasted that he could beat him up. The boast came on the night Sergeant Donaldson refereed a boxing match between the champions of San Felipe and Hermosilla, the nearest village west of San Felipe. Jaime had made the boast because he felt proud that the champion of his town had beaten Hermosilla's champion, and because his own blood had risen during the course of the fight. So Sergeant Donaldson explained it to me. Also, Jaime probably did not think that Sergeant Donaldson would hear of his boast.

But another boy, Ernesto, heard Jaime talking and informed Sergeant Donaldson who regarded Jaime's boast as a taunt and grew angry. He was not able to tell me why he became so angry with Jaime except to say that it was important for him to present a front to the villagers or they would not respect him. I did not accept this thinking, for he could not tell me why they would lose respect for him if he did not offer a front.

I think now that, being barely out of adolescence himself, he responded to an adolescent's threat with all the insecurity of the adolescent. I think also that because he was one of only a handful of North Americans in a village of two hundred fifty, and probably already felt himself almost alone in this place where he was the alien owing not only to nationality but to race, Jaime's taunt may have promoted his sense of isolation and, thus, fear.

Too, while Sergeant Donaldson did not speak of color in telling me this story, the fact is that he was a white *yanqui* in a small collection of mostly white North Americans in an almost entirely black village. (One always assumes that where race is concerned, Americans, like Europeans, think and experience their emotions under this burden.) Perhaps Sergeant Donaldson believed he could not afford the loss of status Jaime's boast implied, so used anger to reestablish some distance between himself and the boy, and, by extension, the village.

But I did not reason in this way then, for although I had lived with Americans for almost three years by the time I met Sergeant Donaldson, I did not know them well enough to see their hearts at work behind their words. Even though I was suspicious of Sergeant Donaldson's manner of thinking, or at least the way in which he expressed it, I did not know what to do with my suspicions. I was not much older than Sergeant Donaldson and I, too, was ignorant.

He said that Jaime came to his house the day after the boxing match, as he did almost every day. Sergeant Donaldson told him that he had heard what Jaime had been saying and that, if Jaime liked, he, Sergeant Donaldson, would fight him, with or without gloves, so that Jaime could prove his ability.

Jaime said he did not want that. He said he had just been having fun by talking about himself as if he were big. Sergeant Donaldson said he understood, but didn't like Jaime's boasting at his expense. He then turned his back to Jaime and ignored him until he left.

In the evening the Guardia corporal came by. He and Sergeant Donaldson were friends because both were soldiers and because Sergeant Donaldson had cleaned the corporal's revolver, giving it the first oiling it had received since the corporal ran out of oil for it months before. After that time, the corporal brought his revolver to Sergeant Donaldson weekly for him to clean and oil. The corporal's inability to keep his weapon clean and free from rust had become a joke between them, though the lack of oil and solvent was the problem rather than the corporal's neglect.

This evening the corporal talked about his wives. The

wife in San Felipe was his favorite. She was a schoolteacher. Sergeant Donaldson understood that the corporal's love for his wife in San Felipe was based on respect. The corporal also had a wife in Hermosilla. He liked her very much when he spent the night in that town, but did not often think of her when he was apart from her. He had two children by her and two by his wife in San Felipe. He also had a child by a woman in Colón. She was his third wife. When he went to Colón, as he did infrequently on affairs for the Guardia, he stayed with her.

Now the corporal asked about Jaime. Was it true that Sergeant Donaldson told Jaime that he would fight him with or without gloves? Sergeant Donaldson said that it was true. The corporal asked if Sergeant Donaldson wanted him to send Jaime away from San Felipe. Sergeant Donaldson was surprised.

"No," he said. "It isn't a serious matter."

Because, the corporal said, he could not permit trouble to occur in this town. If Jaime had misbehaved, the corporal could send him away.

"No, no, no," Sergeant Donaldson said. It wasn't at all necessary. There had been a misunderstanding, that was all. Everything would be fine between Jaime and himself.

The corporal was skeptical but said he was pleased that there was no trouble between Jaime and Sergeant Donaldson, because Jaime had made trouble before and he, the corporal, had had to send him to live with his mother in Colón. He had been gone for a year and the corporal did not think Colón had done him any good. It had taught him to lie with greater conviction, but it had not taught him anything else. Although Jaime was difficult, the corporal did not want to send him to Colón again.

Sergeant Donaldson agreed that Jaime should not go to Colón. He told the corporal that he would talk to Jaime tomorrow. He was certain that everything would be fine between them, between Jaime and himself.

The corporal smiled without reservation and told Sergeant Donaldson that he had made him very happy by saying that. He left his revolver with Sergeant Donaldson and said he would return for it tomorrow.

The next day Sergeant Donaldson talked with Jaime about Colón. Jaime feared the city and did not want to return to it. Sergeant Donaldson and he made up their misunderstanding and when the corporal returned in the evening, Sergeant Donaldson was able to tell him that everything was fine between Jaime and himself and they had enjoyed themselves playing basketball that afternoon.

All of this Sergeant Donaldson told me as our friendship deepened. He told me, too, about the hunters.

On his first stay in San Felipe, he brought a rifle with him, a slide-action, .22-caliber Winchester. He had used it to hunt rabbits in the deserts of California but had not fired it since coming to Panama until he went upriver one day with the corporal to shoot birds. He shot three: a kingfisher, a tree duck, and a bird neither he nor the corporal had a name for. When they returned to the village, the corporal gave the birds to his wife to prepare as food and told his neighbors that Sergeant Donaldson was a very good shot with a rifle. In this way the village learned that he owned a rifle.

Two men, brothers, came to Sergeant Donaldson's house to admire the Winchester. The men were hunters who spent much of their lives upriver where they shot pig and tapir.

They sold the meat in San Felipe and Hermosilla and other villages along the Atlantic coast so they could buy more bullets and gasoline for their outboard so they could go back into the mountains. They asked Sergeant Donaldson if he had any bullets he would sell them, explaining that bullets were expensive in both San Felipe and Hermosilla. Sergeant Donaldson gave them part of a box of bullets, refusing to accept the hunters' money for them.

Several days later, some boys came to his house. They wanted him to get his rifle and cross the river with them. *Un monstruo* was in a tree, they said, and they wanted him to shoot it. They were very excited. Sergeant Donaldson had heard people refer to the anaconda as *un monstruo*, and children sometimes called sharks *monstruos*, but he could not guess what kind of monster would be in a tree. The tide was out and he and the boys waded across the riverbed without difficulty.

On the other side they climbed up the bank and stopped where a number of adults and children were standing. They pointed into the labyrinth of sun and shadow made by the branches of a mahogany tree and the heavy woody vines that hung from them. At first Sergeant Donaldson did not see the animal, so well was it camouflaged, but also because he was looking for a snake. It was not a snake but an iguana, its skin dappled with the colors of the leaves where the sun struck it, but dark, almost black, where it lay concealed by shade. It lay motionless on a thick branch. Sergeant Donaldson loaded his rifle, aimed and fired. He heard the bullet make a hollow *thunk!* as it struck. The iguana did not move. One of the hunters came up beside Sergeant Donaldson. Sergeant Donaldson tried to think of the words in Spanish that would mean "Spot for me" but could not find them. He fired again. The same *thunk!* sound came.

"Did I hit the branch?" he asked the hunter.

The hunter did not think so.

"I'll aim higher. Maybe I'm hitting the branch."

This time there was no sound of the bullet striking. He aimed where he had before and fired several more times, each time the bullet making that *thunk!* It did not sound as if it were striking something solid and reluctant to give, but as though it was hitting something with a resistant surface and then passing through it. But the iguana did not move.

Finally Sergeant Donaldson had used all of his bullets. He told the people who had been watching that he had no more. They had been watching him shoot and they had been making fun of him because the iguana had not moved. Now they started toward the river to return to the village and they laughed openly. When Sergeant Donaldson described this to me I remembered how he had reacted when Jaime had boasted about being able to beat him up, and I imagined how humiliated he must have felt now.

But the hunter told him to wait while his brother went to get more bullets, and because Sergeant Donaldson waited, others turned back and waited too.

The other hunter came and gave Sergeant Donaldson four bullets. Sergeant Donaldson aimed at the iguana's shoulder and pressed the trigger of his rifle. Again there was the sound of the bullet hitting and entering.

"What do you think?" he asked the hunter who had given him the bullets.

"Shoot again in the same place."

Sergeant Donaldson aimed at where the heart would be

and fired. He did the same with the last two rounds. One of the hunters put his hand on Sergeant Donaldson's shoulder. The other only shrugged.

Then the iguana fell out of the tree.

Sergeant Donaldson and the hunters cut through the surge of people to where the iguana lay. Its body was about three feet long, its tail as long as its body. Sergeant Donaldson counted eleven holes in the iguana where a bullet had passed through it; there was no blood. The hunters were grinning.

A boy tied the largest toes of the iguana's front feet into a knot, and then the largest toes of the iguana's rear feet, and then passed the tail through the legs and used the end of it as a carrying handle. Everybody went back across the river. The tide was coming in and people were serious about crossing and watched for sharks. When they were behind the infirmary, one of the hunters told the boy carrying the iguana to untie it. Unbound, the iguana lay on its belly. Everyone waited for Sergeant Donaldson to decide how to divide the meat. Then the iguana began to move. At first Sergeant Donaldson thought its movement was a neural response to death. But then it became clear that it was moving with purpose. It was trying to escape. Sergeant Donaldson drew his knife from its sheath and jammed it into the iguana's neck. It caught in the bone and stuck, but the animal kept moving. It was going toward the river. One of the hunters ran off and returned with the Guardia corporal's revolver. He fired it into the iguana's head. It flattened out on its belly, its legs splayed, its mandible pressed to the earth.

Sergeant Donaldson worked his knife until it came loose. He told his houseboy's mother that all he wanted was one supper from the iguana and that she could have the rest of the meat. After he made this announcement, people began to drift away.

Only later, after he returned to the Canal Zone, did it occur to him that he should have given the hunters some meat in return for the bullets they gave him and for killing the iguana. This violation of obligation weighed on him so that when he knew he would be returning to San Felipe he perhaps went further than necessary in buying two cases of .22-caliber ammunition to give to them.

"But why Abrilio's mother?" I asked. "What did she have to do with the iguana?"

"With the iguana? *Nada.* But she has thirteen children and a husband who is dying of tuberculosis. She's thirty-one years old and has lost all but a few of her teeth. You saw her. She's the woman I gave the perfume to when we came in. Not Elena—the other one." A burst of laughter suddenly issued from him. "God, that was embarrassing. Anyway, I thought it would be a good idea to help her out a little."

I remembered the woman. So she was Abrilio's mother. Sergeant Donaldson said something next that explained her fondness for him, aside from the meat from the iguana.

"When I was here before, I bought a lottery ticket. I did not think it had a chance of winning, so I gave it to Abrilio to give to his mother. Well, it did win. A hundred dollars. When the boy from the store I bought it from came to give me the money, I sent him over to her house. After all, it was her ticket now. Then she tried to return it to me, but I refused to take it. Because it was her ticket. I wasn't being generous; I had given it to her. And while a hundred dollars wasn't much to me, it was a lot to her. I mean, it was like a year's wages to her. So word got around the village. Lieutenant Washington came by and told me what a great piece of public relations I'd done, as if it was something I'd planned. What a fucking idiot. Sorry, sir, I forgot you're an officer."

I made a waving motion with my hand, as though his comment about Lieutenant Washington was unimportant. In a sense, it was; I also had forgotten that I was an officer. What had startled me was his addressing me as "sir."

"Tell me, sir, what would you have done in my place? I'm asking you because one of the medics who was here then gave me a hard time for having given the money away. That was how he saw it."

"Why did he give you a hard time?"

"I don't know. But he felt very strongly that the money should have been mine." He studied me for a moment before continuing. "You know that girl they call Niña? She's a friend of Elena's. He got into her pants and bragged about it. I don't know what that has to do with anything, but it popped into my head. Anyway, Niña is the reason he's not here anymore. You didn't answer my question, sir. What would you have done in my place?"

I thought about this for at least a minute before saying, "I don't think I would have given her the ticket in the first place."

When Sergeant Donaldson remained silent, I said, "In my country there are so many poor people that you stop seeing them. They are simply part of the landscape. Part of the city street."

Sergeant Donaldson nodded. "There are many poor here too."

I agreed. "If there were fewer, you could feel that one

hundred dollars would do something."

"Well, it did something for her."

VI

There was little for me to do to pass the time in San Felipe. Though I was supposed to be Lieutenant Washington's student, his "understudy," neither of us took this relationship seriously. In any case, he was seldom around for me to observe.

Once Elena, Sergeant Donaldson's friend, invited me to lunch at her house. I did not understand that she was merely being polite to me, or perhaps was imitating the manners of North Americans as she understood them, and so at eleven-thirty I presented myself at her house. The occasion became one of terrible embarrassment for her father, who had not expected me, and for me too. He sent Elena to one of the stores to buy another Coke, and everybody—he, Elena, her small brother—gave up a portion of their food so that I could eat too.

The house consisted of two rooms, the living and dining area where Elena and her brother presumably slept at night—two sleeping mats lay rolled behind the open door—and a room built into the far corner with unfinished planks where I assumed their father slept. There was no indication that an adult woman lived there, but I knew by then that Elena's mother had left her family to live in Colón where she became a prostitute. Sergeant Donaldson told me this, and also that Elena, unhappy in the village after her mother left, had lived in Colón with her mother for two years before returning home. She and Jaime had come back to San Felipe at the same time.

As at the home of the English-speaking prostitute I had made love with in Colón, the walls of the house were decorated with photographs of North American celebrities cut from magazines—film and television stars mostly, but also the wife of the United States president who had been assassinated not long before; she was considered by many to be a woman of unusual beauty and high culture. I was reminded of my own village such that the sense of loss I believed I had put behind me shortly after leaving my parents' house for what I was certain would be the remainder of my life came welling up out of my heart and poured from my eyes before I was able to stifle it. I was humiliated, not for myself so much as for my hosts. My command of Spanish left me when the memory of my natal village and my parents' house and my parents showed itself to me, and I said nothing. I could only imagine what Elena and her father must be thinking and feeling as they watched my tears drop into the rice on my plate. They were silent and I left as soon as I could politely do so. I never returned to their house and spoke to them on the street only when not to speak would have been an act of discourtesy. For their part, I was sure that they took my unhappiness as a personal affront to their hospitality, a denigration of their effort to please me.

As if the grief I had just experienced were a foretelling, I found, when I went back to my own house, a message on my cot that my father had died almost two weeks earlier and that my family had already had the funeral. A note from Sergeant Donaldson accompanied the message, saying, "Let me know if there is anything I can do."

My father had suffered from a weak heart all of his life and had never been a strong man, either physically or in terms of personality. Still, it had never occurred to me that he would die before he was fifty. I wanted to ask Sergeant Donaldson to do something for me, but I didn't know what to ask for.

At the edge of the village on the side facing the river where a layer of asphalt had been put down for the landing pad, a pole and hoop had been set up and Sergeant Donaldson and I often played half-court basketball there with some of the boys and younger men from the village. One Saturday I heard the shouts and laughter of a game and went outside, intending to join in. A man I had not seen before was playing with several of the boys with whom I played regularly. Sergeant Donaldson stood at the edge of the court, watching the game. When one of the players took the ball to the foul line for a free throw, Sergeant Donaldson stepped onto the pad. Seeing him take up his position, the others stopped the play, spoke rapidly among themselves, and left the court. Alone, Sergeant Donaldson shot three or four baskets. I walked onto the court and offered to play, but he shook his head no and returned to his house, leaving the ball on the court. He did not look at me and for a moment I felt the humiliation I knew he must have been feeling. I returned to my own house. Soon I heard the noise of the game resume.

The following Monday I looked out my window toward the sounds of a new game and saw Sergeant Donaldson at play with the very boys who had shunned him two days before, as if the shunning had never occurred. But that evening, while I was drinking a Pepsi with him, the Guardia corporal came to visit and Sergeant Donaldson asked him what had happened on Saturday. The corporal was embarrassed and reluctant to answer, but Sergeant Donaldson persisted.

The corporal asked if he had noticed the large man who wore a mustache.

Sergeant Donaldson had.

"He is from this town," the corporal said. "He has been away for five years, working for the *gringos* in the Zone. Maybe twice each year he returns home to visit his mother. He works in the quarry near the canal. He makes the explosions. Boom!"

I did not understand everything the corporal said. I understood that the man with the mustache had learned to hate *gringos*, but I was not certain what to make of the corporal's emphasis on explosives. I did not know whether to assume that Sergeant Donaldson had been threatened or that *gringos* generally should be wary of this man. I find it interesting to recall that it did not occur to me then that I may have been under threat, for, if I was not Panamanian, neither did I see myself as a *gringo*. And, because the corporal spoke to Sergeant Donaldson but not to me, I did not view myself as sharing his situation in the village. While everybody knew Sergeant Donaldson, it was as though, in the eyes of most villagers, I did not exist.

At last Sergeant Donaldson said to the corporal, "But you and I are still friends. Yes?" and extended his hand. The corporal clasped Sergeant Donaldson's hand in both of his own and laughed. There was such release in the laugh that one could almost forget the man who had grown angry in the rock quarry. Even so, I could see the embarrassment that lingered in the corporal's eyes.

Four years earlier, the story went, fifty Cubans put in at San Felipe in small rubber boats, guided there by a man from Hermosilla. I did not understand what happened next— what the Cubans did or said, what the villagers did or said; the story was mixed with a sense of suppressed rage, and while I knew that key points were being left out in the telling, I did not know, and did not think I could find out, what these points were—but four young men, boys actually, lined themselves up in the street to face the Cubans. Each young man carried a .22 caliber rifle, which four rifles comprised all of the firearms in the village save those brought by the Cubans. The Cubans shot the young men and took their rifles. Then they took several young women—girls, including Elena and Niña—into the jungle. Some of the young women returned after two or three days. The others were not seen again.

The Cubans eventually returned, pursued by the Guardia, but they stayed in San Felipe only long enough to recover the boats they had hidden or to be captured by their pursuers. Those who paddled out to sea did so in the attempt to find the yacht that was their mother ship. Perhaps some of them accomplished this; at least they did not come back. Others turned back and were also captured. Only one man was killed this time, and he was the man from Hermosilla who had brought the Cubans to San Felipe. His body washed up on the reef the day after the last Cuban, barring those who escaped, was captured. It is possible that he drowned while trying to get back to the yacht from which the Cubans had launched their invasion. It is possible that the Cubans, for their own reasons, killed him. The story went that nobody knew how he died, although everybody hoped that the villagers of San Felipe had had something to do with his death.

Now the Guardia corporal said that some Communists— Panamanian Communists this time—would be coming to San Felipe. The Communists wanted the *gringos* to leave.

Sergeant Donaldson asked where these Communists were from. The corporal said that while some of them were from Hermosilla, others were from San Felipe. Elena's brother, the older one, would be among them. He lived in Hermosilla now, though of course he had been born in San Felipe. Elena's brother was the only Communist he specified and he mentioned him in a way that indicated the corporal knew all there was to know about Sergeant Donaldson's relationship with Elena. The corporal asked Sergeant Donaldson and Sergeant Lawrence and me to stay indoors while the Communists were in San Felipe, as they had announced their intention to stone the *gringos*. As Lieutenant Washington was away—I had not seen him in several days—I moved in with Sergeant Donaldson and Sergeant Lawrence.

Late in the afternoon we noticed a group of five young men standing at the edge of the village near the river. They stared back at us. They seemed undecided as to what to do.

"They are very young to have studied everything it's necessary to study in order to become a Communist," Sergeant Donaldson said.

I shifted my eyes to him. I thought he might be joking, but he was not. The skin on his face, in fact, was taut with tension. I did not know what he meant, as I did not know what he thought it was necessary to study to be a Communist. In my own country, you enlisted in the party, or at least its military arm, because you were a patriot, or because something terrible had been done to you or your family by those in government or allied with it, or because you were coerced. If you took lessons in how to be a Communist, you took them later.

We recognized Elena's brother. He had only one leg and walked with a hand-carved crutch. He was seventeen, her twin. One of the boys with him had clubfeet and walked with two crutches.

"Think of the determination that kid must have to have walked here from Hermosilla on those sticks," Sergeant Lawrence said.

Another young man was apparently blind and kept his hand on the shoulder of a fourth boy. There seemed to be nothing infirm about either the fourth or the fifth boy, although the latter could not have been more than thirteen or fourteen years old.

"He must be with the others for reasons other than ideological," Sergeant Donaldson said of this one.

"Do you think they all might be with one another for reasons that are not ideological?" I suggested.

"Maybe he's the brother of one of the others," Sergeant Lawrence said, as though he had not heard me.

After a while the Guardia corporal went up to them. He spoke with them and then they followed him to the cantina three houses from ours, near the plaza. Far into the night we heard a loud but unintelligible discussion issue from the cantina. It was still going on when I slipped into my sleeping bag cover. Sergeant Donaldson was already lying on his cot. "Wake me if they stone us," he said to Sergeant Lawrence. Sergeant Lawrence was looking out a window at the street where nothing moved but the occasional dog trotting by or scratching itself.

"I will," he said. Again I could not determine if he and Sergeant Donaldson were joking.

In the morning the Guardia corporal came to tell us that everything was okay: the Communists had returned to Hermosilla, Elena's brother with them. The corporal said he told the people in the village that they should be grateful to the *gringos* for having built the canal, for creating jobs. And he asked them if they wanted the Cubans to come back. Without the *gringos*, they would see the Cubans again, so they should be grateful that the *gringos* put their soldiers in San Felipe. Even those snake eaters from Hermosilla should be grateful. So the corporal told them.

One evening, with the men from the village, Sergeant Donaldson and I hunted lobsters on the reef. When the tide came in we took flashlights and walked the reef until we saw the eyes of a lobster reflecting red light back at us. Then one of us snatched it with his free hand before it could withdraw into its hole. That was all they could do to save themselves—try to pull back into a hole in the reef before we grabbed them. Their claws were tiny and they could not fight us. As long as the light each of us carried did not waver, and the movement of our hands was smooth, they were spellbound, enthralled by the light, and lost to themselves.

We caught almost ninety lobsters that night. The women

boiled them in immense kettles. Then we all, men and women, hunters and cooks, ate the tails hot between gulps of beer. Even now I remember the sensation of biting into that steaming sweet meat and then filling my mouth with bitter beer to cool it. And I can still smell that boiled sea smell that I swallowed down with each bite of lobster.

The only other part of that night I remember now occurred when we were just beginning to walk out on the reef. A small shark came in with a wave and a man with a machete slapped at it with the flat of the knife as it passed behind us. For a moment we all stopped to determine whether or not it would swim back toward us, but we lost it in the dark and soon enough we turned our faces to the open sea again and walked out to where the lobsters were.

In the afternoon of a very hot day, an elderly man, unknown to anyone, walked into the village and up the steps of the infirmary and collapsed just inside the threshold. His pulse was thirty-six. Because he was unconscious, the medics could not question him. Because no one knew him, they did not know what ailed him, so they did nothing but lay him on a bed in the examining room.

The old man slept through the night and in the morning awoke refreshed. His pulse was near sixty. He was from a village two days away, he said. He thought he was eighty-five or eighty-six years old. He told the medics he had been climbing a coconut palm to get the fruit but had suddenly felt weak. He had heard that the North Americans had a clinic in San Felipe, so had walked here in the hope that they had a medicine that would make him feel strong again. One of the medics gave him some small, round candies that looked like pills and instructed him on how often to take one. The old man tried one but did not like the taste of it and returned the others to the medic. He left for his home village the following morning. His pulse was at sixty-eight, his blood pressure one-ten over seventy. Perhaps he had just needed a rest, he said. He laughed at the silliness his body had put him through.

Early one evening, as the tide was going out, the village nearly emptied itself of adults who crossed the river and disappeared into the forest. Elena went with them but Jaime stayed back. I asked him what was going on and he said he did not know. When I started after them, he grabbed my shirt and said I couldn't go; the North Americans had to stay in the village. I stared at him and then made to go after the other villagers again. "No!" he said, and grabbed me again. "It's bad!" Then he said, so quietly that I almost did not hear him: "They are going to kill chickens."

At first I thought he was talking about them as food, perhaps for a common pot. There were chickens all over the village; they wandered freely, as did dogs and even a few hairy pigs. But why would people have to go into the forest to kill them?

An older boy who was being trained by the medics came out of the infirmary and stood beside Jaime. Jaime said, "Tell him."

"It's religion," the older boy said. "It's bad."

I began to understand then what was going on. "Did the *brujo* come?" I had been told by the Guardia corporal that a *brujo* lived alone about an hour outside the village toward the mountains. The corporal considered him a bad man, but one that was very powerful. He had had two horses and when the Cubans were here they killed one of them. In retaliation, he did something to the Cubans so that even before the Guardia Nacional found them, some had already died. This story was at odds with the other story the corporal had told us about the Cubans, in which none had died, but I did not challenge him.

"Yes," the boy said. The *brujo* was in the forest on the other side of the river.

I thanked him and then thanked Jaime for warning me. I assured him that I would stay in the village and I saw his body ease and he smiled.

The three of us sat down on the steps of the infirmary and watched the empty street. After a minute or two, the older boy went inside. Jaime asked me: "You know the girl who lives there?" He turned his face toward Elena's house but did not point at it.

"Elena?" I said.

"You like her?"

I looked at him. "Yes," I said, hoping he did not mean anything more than friendship.

"You want her?"

I looked at him again.

"You can have her. You want me to tell her you want her?"

"No," I said. I stood up and crossed the street to my house.

Within the hour the people returned from across the

river. They were quiet and looked tired. They went to their houses without speaking either to one another or to me as I sat by my window, watching them.

Sergeant Lawrence returned from the river still wet from swimming. I was waiting for Sergeant Donaldson to finish a radio transmission so we could play basketball. Some of the boys were already on the court.

"You know that girl, Elena?" Sergeant Lawrence asked me.

"Yes."

"She just bit me on the dick."

I did not allow myself to look at Sergeant Donaldson. He was wearing earphones, so perhaps he had not heard.

"I was out on the river, hanging on my air mattress, and she swam out and dived down and the next thing I know she's got her teeth on my dick. I thought a shark had it. Then she bobs up and she's laughing. '*El monstruo*,' she says. Then she puts her hand in my trunks."

"A little shark. For a little dick," Sergeant Donaldson said. To me, he said, "Come on. Let's play some basketball."

Sergeant Lawrence said, "Hey, it's not that little! Besides, I was swimming."

I have mentioned Lieutenant Washington. I did not know him well. I seldom saw him, nor did the other Americans. On occasion the Guardia corporal asked about him in such a way that I knew he already knew the answer, but wanted to know if I was aware of Lieutenant Washington's activities. There were stories we heard from some of the villagers about parties he had with women whose husbands were away at sea, fishing. Ultimately, the lieutenant's behavior became such an embarrassment that the American command considered withdrawing all of its soldiers from San Felipe. So I was informed by the command sergeant major several months later, shortly before my departure from Panama.

In fact, the North Americans who resided in the village were withdrawn and replaced by a different contingent. I imagine this occurred so that Lieutenant Washington could be removed without the command accepting responsibility for his behavior even as it tried to contain the damage he had caused. Headquarters could say, if asked, that our recall owed simply to a scheduled rotation of soldiers in and out of San Felipe.

This happened following a visit by a staff officer, a Major Boren, from our group. On a Friday morning, he came in unannounced with the helicopter that delivered medical supplies. He was a large man who referred to himself as a bear, although most of his weight was around his hips and in his middle. Had it not been for the strength of his voice and his position on staff, he would have been considered obese in the way women get obese, but, as it was, younger officers feared him.

When the helicopter set down, he was the first to disembark, handing a medical kit to one of the medics who had run out to the landing pad. The crew chief then began unloading the crated supplies, and the medics and the boys and girls they were training lugged them to the infirmary. The major waited at the edge of the landing pad until the helicopter was secured and the crew chief and the pilots had joined him, and then they walked to the plaza where the mayor and

the school teachers and the Guardia corporal and Lieutenant
Washington greeted him. When the pilots, whom we knew,
passed us, Sergeant Donaldson and Sergeant Lawrence and
me, they did not look at us and we knew then that something impended.

After an hour or so, the major came alone to my house.
I offered him coffee from a small stove I had built from a C-
ration can, but he declined. He asked why I hadn't gone to
the plaza with Lieutenant Washington and the village lead-
ers earlier. I did not have an answer. I had not gone because
it had not occurred to me to go, but I could not say that.
I apologized and said I had not known there would be a
ceremony.

"I realize your position with us is somewhat ambiguous,
but for everybody's benefit, you should pretend you're one of
us. You're wearing our uniform, after all."

"Yes, sir."

"Lieutenant Washington thinks you spend too much
time with the NCOs."

I did not say anything. There was nothing I could say.

"For me, that's not a problem. They're the ones who make
the army go, after all, and it's good to get to know them and
to know how they do things. When I was a young second
lieutenant in Burma, I quickly realized how little they needed me, but how much I needed them."

He hesitated, then said, "I've been hearing stories about
Lieutenant Washington. Not only *I*, but *we*. We at Fort Gulick. Is there anything you'd like to tell me?"

When, again, I did not say anything, he said, "Your name
doesn't pop up, except for the fact that you're here. Lieutenant Washington's, on the other hand... I realize that your

loyalty, your oath of allegiance, is to your own army and your own country, not to ours, but you are attached to us, and you have made friends among us... I understand that you and Lieutenant Washington don't get along."

"I do not know how Lieutenant Washington regards me, but I do not dislike him. I have seen him perhaps eight times in the weeks I have been here. I did not know him at Fort Gulick."

"Eight times? Doesn't he live here too?"

I swallowed, and said: "Yes, but he is not often here. When he is here, I often absent myself. I stay with the NCOs then." Then I said: "I also have heard stories about Lieutenant Washington's activities. I do not want people to tell stories about me."

"I wish you had told us, Lieutenant."

"I was not sure that I had the... the..."

Major Boren waited as I stumbled, searching for the word that was lost in the jumble of my English vocabulary. Finally I said, "I did not know if you would believe me." It was not exactly what I wanted to say, but it was close.

The major's eyebrows raised. He said, "You're not in any trouble, Lieutenant. You can set your mind at ease on that count." He drew in his breath. "Well. We're going lobster hunting on the reef tonight. I assume you'll join us. Have you done that yet?"

"Yes, sir," I said, answering his question.

"Good. I'll see you when we get together then. Dusk, I suppose. Where do the radio operators live? That way?"

"Yes, sir. The next house in that direction."

He stood. "Thank you, Lieutenant. You've been very helpful."

Five minutes later I heard shouting. I looked out a window and saw Major Boren berating Sergeant Donaldson and Sergeant Lawrence in the street in front of their house. "… attracts flies!" the major was saying. "And flies have shit on their feet! You don't see it but it's there! You keep garbage in your house and they come from that pile of dog shit they've been feeding at to your house and they walk all over every fuckin' thing, your food, your face, tracking shit everywhere. When I was in Burma every man in the Marauders got dysentery, and it was because of those fuckin' flies that followed us everywhere. They're too little to shoot and too many to poison, so you've got to keep them away from you. Now get that garbage out of your house."

"If we put it outside, the dogs will get into it, sir," Sergeant Lawrence said.

"You're sergeants in the American army. I'm sure you'll figure out a way to get it out of your house *and* keep the dogs from getting it. Where's the sump? There must be a sump in this place."

"Down by the latrines, sir, at the other end of the village."

"All right. So what you do is, every time one of you goes to take a leak, you take your garbage with you, if there is any, and dump it in the sump. That shouldn't be so hard."

"Yes, sir," said Sergeant Lawrence.

"Yes, sir," said Sergeant Donaldson.

When the major had gone, Sergeant Lawrence said, "What do we do about the flies that get on us when we're taking a shit? I mean they've definitely been walking on shit."

"I dare you to go and ask him," Sergeant Donaldson said.

"I say we shoot 'em. They're not that small. We'll line

'em up against the latrine wall and blast 'em. We'll do it by tens. Get ten men from the village, give them rifles and make executioners out of them. I know what you're gonna say: How do we keep those fuckin' little flies still while the executioners are taking aim? The answer is: we chloroform them first. See? I'm a sergeant in the American army and I found a solution."

"Better get his persimmon first."

"His persimmon?"

"Well, he's not going to give you his permission to execute flies. He'd have to approve your handing out weapons to foreign nationals. He's not going to do that."

"You're nuts. I think all those stories they tell about you are true."

"What stories?"

"No stories. I just made that up."

"What stories?"

"Really, I just made that up. I'm sorry I said it."

"All right."

"Sorry, man."

"All right."

The lobster hunt went much as it had the first time I went, but we went into the water at a different place on the reef. Here there was a sand beach where the wooden frames of a number of small boats rested. The moon was full and in its light the boats' skeletons shined as though they had been polished with a rubbing cloth. Major Boren, physically an awkward man—one wondered how he had done in the jungles of Burma, but he probably had not been so fat or so wide when he was young—fell twice and, the second time, had to be pulled to the surface by those walking beside him. Nevertheless, he ended up with more lobsters in his bag than anyone else. It was a mystery not to be contemplated.

We did not catch as many as we did the first time, but we caught enough. The women boiled them and we ate them with beer, listening to the major's reminiscences of the Burma campaign and his recollections of the men he had known there. His feeling for them was genuine, I believe. While he was, or had become, a sentimental man, he did not exaggerate their, or his own, travails in their war against the Japanese. If anything, I thought, he talked about them with understatement. He spoke only in English—perhaps he did not know Spanish—and the villagers who stood around as he talked and ate and drank understood little if anything of what he said, but laughed when they saw the North Americans laugh and looked grim when they saw the North Americans look grim, and Major Boren talked on through the night.

He left at mid-morning the next day. The pole that supported the basketball hoop was replaced at the end of the landing pad as soon as the helicopter had gone and five minutes later half a dozen village boys and Sergeant Donaldson and I were playing basketball. I did not see Major Boren again, but several years later I learned that he was part of what the Americans called the Studies and Observation Group, which conducted clandestine operations in northern Viet Nam as well as in Laos and Cambodia.

When we learned that we were to be withdrawn from San Felipe, Sergeant Donaldson said, "Nothing lasts forever." He was alluding to his relationship with Elena, which surprised me because only two weeks earlier he had entertained the notion of deserting from the army so as to remain in San Felipe in order to be near her.

The Guardia corporal had encouraged this fantasy, suggesting that he and Sergeant Donaldson could build up a fishing fleet and sell their catch in the villages along the Atlantic coast. Years before, another North American had lived here. He had built a fleet of fifteen boats but finally he grew old and died, and now the boats rotted in the jungle. The corporal knew where they were. He and Sergeant Donaldson could make them seaworthy again; they could make a lot of money with them. I asked if the remains of boats I had seen on the beach where we went after the lobsters were part of the dead North American's fleet. The corporal laughed— it was at the way I had spoken of the North American as "dead," he said, but I did not understand what I had said or how I had said it that was funny. When he finished laughing, the corporal said yes, those boats had been part of the fleet, but they were beyond repair now. Still, he knew where the others were.

Jaime, too, wanted Sergeant Donaldson to stay in San Felipe. He had heard about the war the North Americans were fighting and did not want Sergeant Donaldson to go there.

"Which war?" Sergeant Donaldson asked, as though the United States were fighting so many he could not be certain to which Jaime referred. His face wore an expression of genuine puzzlement.

"In Asia. On the other side of the world," Jaime said.

Sergeant Donaldson turned to me. "Are we at war in Asia again?"

"I don't know. I've been in this village as long as you have."

It was possible that US military activities on the peninsula or elsewhere had escalated into full-scale warfare, but I did not think that likely, especially as Major Boren and the helicopter crewmen had said nothing about it. I was inclined, rather, to think that Jaime had heard something on the radio about the Peninsular War, perhaps an historical analysis, and had confused this with the events of our own day. This is probably what happened, for when Sergeant Donaldson and the other North Americans and I returned to Fort Gulick, we were able to ascertain that, indeed, there was no war, or at least nothing the United States was involved in that was large enough to be called a war. Yet, eerily, Jaime's error seemed to presage something, for even as he spoke about a war in Asia, I felt the air grow cold as though filled with death and terror and more death beyond quantifying. It was as though once the words had been released, they manufactured their own truth.

Jaime, not knowing what to make of Sergeant Donaldson's bewilderment, asked, "Do you want to go there?"

Sergeant Donaldson thought. For him, if not for Jaime, it was a hypothetical question. "I don't know," he said finally. When Jaime's expression did not change, Sergeant Donaldson, with all of the romantic fatalism of the warrior, said, "I am a soldier. I go where they tell me to go." When Jaime continued to stare at him, Sergeant Donaldson, perhaps only to be polite, said, "I would rather stay here."

"Then stay! Don't go to Asia! You will die there!" Jaime threw himself against Sergeant Donaldson in what I thought at first was an assault. But in an instant it was apparent that all Jaime wanted was to hold onto him, to root him here in San Felipe. Jaime was crying. "Don't go! You can hide in the jungle if the *gringos* come. We'll kill them! I don't want you to die!"

Sergeant Donaldson brought his hand up and stroked the back of Jaime's head. He looked uncomfortable, as if he did not know what to do. I was moved: this thin child of African ancestry being caressed by a well-muscled young American of European stock is an image that remains fixed in my memory to this day, obviously. I do not know if anyone took a photo of them; I do not remember which of the other Americans, if any, were present. But it could have been made into an excellent propaganda poster, promoting the American view of their activities in Central America and a number of the Caribbean countries. (Certainly the photo on which the poster would have been based would have to have been doctored, as many Latin Americans, like North Americans, despise, or pretend to despise, homosexual practices, or even innuendos.) Sergeant Donaldson told me the next day that he dreamed that night that he had won the lottery again.

For my own part, I was relieved that he had not deserted. Aside from losing my closest friend, I would have been faced with the moral quandary of not having reported his intention to my superiors as soon as he divulged it to me. As it was, the moral question remained, but I was able to avoid it because he returned with the rest of us to the Canal Zone.

VII

We were on the same LCM that had carried us to San Felipe only a few weeks before. I do not think I spoke to anyone during the time we were at sea. Sergeant Donaldson and I, as if by agreement, ensconced ourselves at opposite ends of the boat. I thought a great deal about Sergeant Lawrence, wondering if he knew about Sergeant Donaldson's relationship with Elena. I decided at last that he did know, and had known before he boasted about his sexual activity with her. I wondered, too, if Sergeant Donaldson had confided his thoughts about desertion to him. Certainly Elena's betrayal, or Sergeant Donaldson's learning of it, served to bind him once again to the army. But had Sergeant Lawrence understood what he was doing when he announced that Elena had put her mouth on his penis? I did not know. I did not know Sergeant Lawrence well enough to decide whether he acted out of instinct or calculation.

Of course, I had seen before how a woman could be used to alter the relations between men. I had observed how women could be agencies by which men dominate one another. And now I had seen how this domination, painful as it was, cemented a soldier's relationship to his fellows.

On this short voyage there was no stopping to kill sharks and we were in the Canal Zone only hours after we left San Felipe. That night I made love with a woman from Medellín. Her thighs were very white and her breasts were as round as apples and her pubic hair smelled of soap. When we had finished she washed herself from a pan of sudsy water. Then she washed me and I became aroused again and we made love for the second time. Afterward I waited for her to put her clothes on and then I walked with her down the stairs to the bar where I had met her.

At the top of the stairs, before starting down, I saw two young women I had seen in the bar earlier. They caressed each other on the bed in a room which door had been left open. They were from Medellín also, the woman with me said. "They love each other."

The very next day I was attached to an operational detachment that would be participating in a training exercise to begin almost immediately. When the Group personnel officer informed me of my assignment I had so strong an impression that he considered it a punishment for my association with Lieutenant Washington, involuntary though it was, that something like dismay must have appeared on my face. He put his hand on my shoulder in what he probably believed was a fatherly gesture, but I was so slight of frame that his large hand landed on my bony shoulder with the force of a falling brick and pained me as such a brick would. "It won't last long," he said. "Ten days. Then it will be over." Which statement, of course, reinforced my feeling that I was being punished.

As it happened, Sergeant Donaldson and I found ourselves once again on the same detachment. If on the return trip from San Felipe we had needed distance from each other (for a reason I, at least, was unable to define), we now gravitated to each other as though we were halves of a single entity and sat side by side during the briefings.

Following the briefings, the detachment was kept isolated from the rest of the company overnight and the next day while it tested its radios, checked out its medical kits, was issued and loaded blank ammunition, packed its gear, and discussed the meaning of the intelligence it had been provided and how to execute its operation order.

That night we paddled across the Canal in rubber boats and met our contact on the opposite shore. We beached our boats and deflated them, then dug a hole in the sand and buried them. We followed our contact to a rendezvous with an American pilot who, according to the scenario, had been shot down and was waiting for us to evacuate him. The darkness of the jungle was so complete that the strips of luminous tape each of us wore on the back of his cap were not visible even to the man immediately behind him. Each soldier grasped the belt of the man in front of him. When one fell he pulled the soldier ahead of him down too, and the man behind stumbled over both. Finally we came to a hilltop that was clear of vegetation. An unpaved road led down the other side. Off the road but still in the clearing was a two-and-a-half-ton truck.

The detachment commander told us to set up a defensive perimeter. However, before we could do this—some men were settling in among the trees and the high grass surrounding the clearing while others, including myself, were trying to locate the outlines of the circle so that we could determine where to place ourselves—the commander told us to get in the back of the truck. Sergeant Donaldson, beside whom I found myself, was reluctant to get into the vehicle. "Something is wrong," he said. When finally everyone who had been in concealment at the edges of the clearing stood up, I realized that we had been positioned so that our perimeter was open on one side: the enemy—"Aggressors," they were called— could slip into our midst and we would not know it until they opened fire.

As everyone else was climbing into the rear of the truck, Sergeant Donaldson did too, and I followed him. Once we were all inside, our contact thanked us for being so cooperative, then informed us that we were prisoners and instructed us to hand out our weapons. We quickly raised the tarp on the sides of the truck and saw that we were indeed surrounded by Aggressor soldiers. I was certain that they had come in behind us where our perimeter was open.

After we gave up our rifles, our contact told us to come out of the truck one person at a time. Sometimes I heard the sounds of scuffling following a man's jumping out, but I did not hear any sound that seemed to issue from pain. When it was my turn, I jumped down out of the truck bed. Hands were on me even before I landed on the ground. I was thrown onto my stomach, my arms jerked up behind me. My wrists were bound with what I knew was parachute suspension line—it was our all-purpose tying material, replacing twine, cord, even string—and a heavy rough rope was twisted around my neck. Finally I was hoisted to my feet. When I turned my head to try to ascertain the positions of the guards as well as the members of my detachment, the rope was yanked tight and not only I but also all of my peers strangled, for the rope was looped around the neck of every prisoner. I felt slack come into the rope again, but the coil around my neck did not loosen to where it had been before. This meant that each time a guard pulled on the rope, I, and the other prisoners, would be strangled a little more by the rope's grip on itself. The guards might not even know that they were killing us.

Behind me, bodies pushed against, or were pushed against, one another. I heard grunts of resistance. Then there was the sharper noise of fists landing on flesh. Somebody yelled, and from my right I heard the cracking and crashing, like an intensity of dry wood breaking, of a man running through the underbrush. At the corner of my vision I saw two men I had not seen before go into the jungle. Soon they returned with Corporal Cobb, one of the members of our team.

His captors placed him in front of me. They unloosed the rope from my neck, circled it once around Corporal Cobb's neck and coiled it again around mine. Then two of the guards began to punch Corporal Cobb. I shouted at them and the guard behind me pulled on the rope, closing my voice off in my throat. When Corporal Cobb fell, the guards kicked him. Then they made him stand up and they marched all of us off the hill, following the dirt road. Corporal Cobb was very short, even shorter than I, and I could see him walking on the balls of his feet because I and the prisoner immediately in front of him were taller and the guards would not let us get close enough to him to permit the rope to slacken. Sometimes the guard foremost in the file or one in the rear pulled on the rope seemingly for no reason other than the fun of it.

This was my first experience with gratuitous cruelty. Although I later witnessed or otherwise learned of atrocities even by soldiers of my own country whom I myself commanded, I have always associated this kind of arbitrary physical barbarity, and the pleasure it afforded at least some of its perpetrators, with the American character. This is unjust, I know. Some men gravitate toward that work which will permit them to satisfy the sadistic qualities in their nature. Others become cruel by force of circumstance and may, in their later lives, put this aspect of themselves aside. Such men are not limited to a single nationality, but show us the terrible parts of ourselves as a species. I know this, yet because I first witnessed this type of cruelty perpetrated by Americans, minor though it was compared with what I was to observe in later years, I continue even now to regard it as definitive of the United States.

When we reached the bottom of the hill an orange dawn was beginning to break up the night clouds and the guards halted us. A man wearing a captain's bars worked his way up the file, stopping at each man. When he came to Sergeant Donaldson—I could see now that the soldier three positions in front of my own on the rope was my friend—the captain asked if he was being choked. Sergeant Donaldson kicked him.

"I'm a doctor," the captain said.

Sergeant Donaldson tried to kick him again, but this time the officer sidestepped the thrust and kicked Sergeant Donaldson in the leg.

"I'm a doctor, goddamnit. I'm trying to help you."

I understood Sergeant Donaldson's point of view. Trained to regard any show of kindness by the enemy as an act of propaganda or deception, Sergeant Donaldson and his fellows were obligated to be wary of and to defend themselves against their enemy and his intentions. And even if this officer was really a medical doctor, the fact that he was moving about unrestrained placed him in the category of "enemy."

Now, however, Sergeant Donaldson opened his mouth as if to speak, but instead of words, his tongue came out of his mouth. It was enormous and once it had pushed itself out, it did not go back in. A squeaking noise issued from his throat.

"Loosen this rope!" the officer shouted at one of the guards. "Goddamnit, take it off them. You're killing these men."

The guards hastened to remove the rope.

"Is that better?" the officer asked.

Sergeant Donaldson nodded his head.

The prisoners were told to sit down at the side of the road. We could see now, with the day's new light, that there were not many guards. It was apparent that they were concerned that some of us might escape. Another officer, a captain I recognized as being on the group's staff, seemed to be in charge of them. I did not know any of the guards and was certain they had been brought in from another unit.

The man who had met our detachment on the beach, our so-called contact, walked along the road with one of the guards. He looked at each of us as though he were weighing us in his mind, as though he were evaluating our individual worth. "You son of a bitch," I heard someone down the line say.

In a moment, the deuce-and-a-half grumbled up from behind us. It proceeded to the head of the column and stopped. The prisoners were ordered back into the truck. One at a time, we placed a foot in the stirrup of the lowered tailgate and were pushed up into the bed of the vehicle by two guards. By the time I had seated myself on one of the wooden benches that folded out from the sides, a senior sergeant named Lopez had his hands free and, with a small clasp knife, was sawing through the nylon suspension line binding the wrists of the man beside him. The latter's hands unbound, he took the knife and cut the line around the wrists of the soldier at his left. Soon Corporal Cobb's hands were free, and then mine. Corporal Cobb, first looking to be sure that no one outside the truck was watching, passed the knife to the man seated opposite him. This man's hands were already loose and he began working at the wrists of the soldier next to him.

When the captain who commanded the guards climbed up into the truck and the tailgate was raised and fastened behind him, everybody's hands were out of sight and the suspension line that had bound us was stuffed into our pockets. Everybody recognized this officer and he knew all of us and we resented his affiliation with our enemy. As he made his way forward to gain sitting space, he shouted to the driver to move out.

The truck was in second gear and accelerating and the captain had not yet sat down. He had just said "I can't think of a finer bunch of men to go to jail with" in a tone weighted with humor and irony, when Corporal Cobb sprang off the bench and drove his head into the base of the captain's spine, propelling him into the wooden fence separating the bed from the truck's cab. Before he could either fall or catch his balance, Sergeant Lopez stuck the point of the blade of the knife under the captain's chin and nicked the skin, drawing a perfectly round bead of blood, a tiny vermilion bubble, and said, "Shut up, motherfucker, or I'll kill you."

Sergeant Lopez was invested in what he was doing. I could see in the set of his mouth and the way the muscles in his face jumped how engaged he was. Another soldier, Specialist Larosa, leaned forward and said to the captain, "I think he means it, sir," and the captain did not say anything more.

The truck was racing now, as if the seasonal road was

an asphalted highway, and the men were shouting, "Jump! Jump!" I looked out the back and estimated that we were doing sixty kilometers an hour. Reluctant to go, I felt the *Jump! Jump!* at my back as an unrelenting pressure and I placed one hand on the tailgate and swung my legs out and dropped. I hit on my feet, bounced back onto my shoulders, rolled with the momentum, came up on my feet again and sat down hard on my rear. In a moment I was able to stand and I ran into the jungle. I ran until I was certain I could not be seen from the road, then, concealing myself behind a tree, I waited and listened.

Soon I heard from the direction I had come the crackling of boots on dry leaves. I peered around the trunk of the tree and saw Sergeant Donaldson tucking himself behind a mango tree. I could not keep myself from smiling, I was so happy to see someone I knew, and better, someone who was my friend. I waved. He saw me and immediately put his finger to his lips. Then he displayed the palm of his hand as a signal to me to stay where I was. In a minute or two, he regained his feet and walked over to my hiding place, stepping very carefully and making almost no noise.

"Someone is in the jungle down by the road," he whispered. "He's walking parallel to it." He picked up a rock and hefted it. It appeared to fit his hand comfortably. He said he intended to take the man's rifle. Together we stalked the sounds the other man's boots made on the dry ground. We were almost within striking distance of the man when I recognized him. "Corporal Cobb."

The small man turned to face us. "What are you going to do with that rock?" he asked. His expression was one of fear and suspicion.

"We thought you were one of the guards," Sergeant Donaldson said. "I was going to take your weapon."

Corporal Cobb opened his mouth to laugh. Sergeant Donaldson held up his hand, hissing: "Shh! Listen!" He motioned to Corporal Cobb to get behind a tree and we quickly got ourselves behind two others.

Men were coming into the forest. There were the boot sounds and now there were two voices. One had seen Corporal Cobb—"the little one"—enter the woods and wanted to pursue him, but the other was hesitant, arguing that more of us than the one his companion had seen had escaped and we could be waiting to ambush them. The second voice prevailed and ultimately the two convinced themselves that we were probably not where we were and they returned to the road.

Sergeant Donaldson was disappointed. He had wanted to hurt at least one of them and he had wanted a rifle.

"They're from that infantry outfit we aggressed against last year," Corporal Cobb said. "We'll get another chance at them sooner or later."

"Sooner or later I'll be somewhere else. I wanted to do something now."

We found ourselves walking.

"What do we do?" Corporal Cobb asked.

"We'll go to the rally point. What else can we do?" Sergeant Donaldson said.

"I don't know."

Sergeant Donaldson laughed. "I didn't expect an answer."

A moment later, he said, "As long as we stay off the roads we'll be all right. They're not going to come into the jungle after us."

"They're afraid of us. Did you hear them talking?" Corporal Cobb giggled.

"You mean when we were waiting to brain them?"

"Yeah." Corporal Cobb giggled again.

"We'll be all right as long as we stay in the jungle."

The first rally point was a rotting dock extending from the shore of a small lake. We waited for an hour without seeing another person before deciding to go to the next rally point. Spotting a wooden pallet among the refuse on the shore, Sergeant Donaldson suggested we build a raft by which to cross the lake. We could put our clothes on the raft and tow it across. When we grew tired we could use it to rest until our strength returned. It would be safer and more direct than walking around the lake. If we walked, we would have to cross the highway, and the Aggressors were certain to be using vehicular patrols.

Corporal Cobb and I agreed.

"Give me your boot laces," Sergeant Donaldson said.

He tore slats of wood out of the dock's platform. He used the laces from our boots and his own and the nylon suspension line we had hidden in our pockets when we were on the truck to fasten the slats to the pallet. While Sergeant Donaldson worked, Corporal Cobb and I watched, and while we watched, Corporal Cobb talked. Neither Sergeant Donaldson nor I paid particular attention to Corporal Cobb's ramblings until he told us that he had once been a master sergeant but had been demoted for killing a soldier he had caught in bed with his wife.

"I shot him," Corporal Cobb said. "I should have shot her too. We were stationed in Texas. I might have gotten away with it. I could have called it a crime of passion. You know, where you kill your wife and the guy she's screwing because you just see red."

"You didn't do time?" Sergeant Donaldson asked.

Corporal Cobb shook his head. "My wife said she was being raped and I shot the guy who was raping her."

"So you got off, but the army busted you anyway."

"They didn't believe me. Officially they had to. But they knew my wife. They knew I'd murdered that kid."

"What excuse did they use to bust you?"

"They found something. They busted me down to sergeant."

But he was a corporal now. Yet neither Sergeant Donaldson nor I asked the obvious question. Instead, Sergeant Donaldson asked, "Are you still married to her?"

"Hell no!"

"Don't tell me you killed her."

Corporal Cobb giggled. "No. I divorced her after the trial was over."

"For adultery?"

"I should have. That would have told them something."

"The raft is ready."

"I'm not sure I can swim that far," Corporal Cobb said.

"Swim as far as you can. You can hang onto the raft when you get tired."

We took off our clothes and placed them on the raft. Then we walked out into the lake, Sergeant Donaldson and Corporal Cobb each grasping a corner of the raft, towing it behind them, I wading out at the rear, pushing the raft with one hand. When the water was deep enough, we began to swim with a one-armed dog paddle. It was midday and the coolness of the water was pleasant and I drank some of it.

"This water has germs in it that are going to eat your guts out before they kill you," Corporal Cobb said cheerily.

Sergeant Donaldson was squinting back toward where we had entered the water. "Look. Next to the dock. See it?"

"What is it?" Corporal Cobb asked.

"I could swear it's an otter. I didn't know there were otters here."

Halfway across, Corporal Cobb said he couldn't swim anymore. Sergeant Donaldson told him to hold onto the raft and we would pull him.

I felt good. The water was serene. I felt as if I could swim all day.

We beached beside another dock. A boat with an outboard motor was tied up to it. We discussed stealing the boat, but decided against it. Although we thought it would be fun, it would not have brought us closer to the second rally point. We disassembled the raft and relaced our boots and put the suspension line in our pockets. Then we walked into the jungle again. Corporal Cobb complained that he was hungry. I did not want to think about my hunger. To think about it made it worse.

We had to cross a road after all. Concealed by foliage, we sat on a hill overlooking the road and watched the traffic.

"See that green pickup?" said Corporal Cobb. "I had one just like it. It even had the same sideview mirrors, the kind you see on those long-haul trucks, those big diesels. I accidentally killed a man with one of those mirrors."

I did not know what to think of Corporal Cobb now. He had killed not one man but two, and neither with the legitimacy provided by war. He was a courageous man; I understood that from his attempt to escape from our captors and from his refusal to complain when they beat him later. But what else was he? To kill two men in separate incidents, claiming one death as resulting from an act performed out of rage and the other as an accident—how could there not be a hidden purpose behind these killings, regardless of his explanations? Here he was, round and elfish and burnt from the sun, sitting beside me. I wished fervently that he would not continue his story. But he went on and in such a way—succinctly and with the sadness of memory—that I was convinced he had killed the second man exactly as he said he had.

On a rainy night Corporal Cobb—then Sergeant Cobb—made a left-hand turn onto a highway, hitting a jogger with the mirror mounted on the passenger door. He had not seen the jogger. This happened in Oklahoma where Sergeant Cobb was stationed after he killed his wife's lover. Because of this second incident, though no charges were brought, the army reduced him in rank to private first class. It took him four years to gain the rank of corporal.

He did not think now that he would ever be promoted again. The rank of sergeant bore too much responsibility. The army had lost faith in his ability to make reasoned judgments. Corporal Cobb himself doubted his ability to dominate the devils that resided in his soul.

Traffic was becoming sparse.

"We'll be able to cross soon," Sergeant Donaldson said.

We waited twenty minutes and then we crept down to where the undergrowth was beginning to thin, a few meters from the road. We lay hidden for five minutes more. Then Sergeant Donaldson said, "Let's go," and we scrambled up the embankment and across the road and were in the forest again in only seconds. But two drivers had blasted their car horns at us before we got across the road.

"So much for stealth and cunning," Sergeant Donaldson said.

Corporal Cobb laughed.

Sergeant Donaldson estimated that the next rally point was less then a kilometer from where we stood. He knew a footpath that led directly to it. I wondered what we would do if we found nobody at this rally point. But soon we stepped off the path into a clearing overhung by second-growth canopy and there were the other members of our team, or at least most of them. Four, including the team commander, the only officer other than myself, had not been able to get off the truck before a second truck closed up behind it, Master Sergeant Stone said. Master Sergeant Stone was the most senior sergeant on our team. We did not see the team commander again for the rest of the exercise.

"Where were you?" Master Sergeant Stone said. "We waited at the dock for almost an hour. Did you go to the dock?"

"Yeah," Sergeant Donaldson said. "We couldn't have missed you by too much. We had to hide from the Aggressors for a while, but that didn't take up too much time."

"Did you see the otter? Just below the dock?"

"Yeah! You saw it too? I thought I was hallucinating."

"You weren't hallucinating. There's a kind of otter they have down here. Its fur isn't as thick as on the one we have in the States."

"So what do we do now? Wait until somebody comes along and tells us?"

"You got something better to do? Captain Dain was here

a few minutes ago. They hadn't counted on us escaping, so he had to go find out what to do with us."

"There's another one for Lopez," Sergeant Donaldson said. Master Sergeant Stone seemed not to understand and Sergeant Donaldson said, "Captains from staff."

"Oh, yeah." Master Sergeant Stone laughed. "Lopez sure gets into it, doesn't he?" He turned his attention to me as I stood at Sergeant Donaldson's elbow.

"Is this your shadow?"

"He's doing all right," Sergeant Donaldson said. "He's learning fast."

"Are you learning a lot, Lieutenant?" Master Sergeant Stone asked.

Like many North Americans, he suffered from xenophobia, and, like many North Americans, used sly insult to keep foreigners at bay. I decided that the easiest action on my part would be to pretend that I was the uncomprehending Asian the master sergeant preferred me to be, and I answered stereotypically with a broad smile: "It's very interesting."

I expected him to turn his attention back to Sergeant Donaldson, but he did not. Instead, he surprised me by persisting: "Is it? But are you learning anything, sir?"

"I am learning very much, thank you," I answered. To deter further humbling, I added "Sergeant" to my response so that it came out: "I am learning very much. Thank you, Sergeant," as though I were dismissing his concern for my education by reminding him of the difference in our statuses.

Actually, I had not intended to sound as peremptory as I believe I did, although, recalling this exchange now, my retort had exactly the effect I had hoped for, and perhaps I intended my curtness after all. In any event, Master Sergeant Stone's eyes opened a little more and he said, "That's real fine, sir." He turned from me then and did not again attempt to overpower me.

Overall, I think he was a good senior sergeant. He cared for his subordinates and they respected him. I think his xenophobia was a function of his love for his own kind and his desire to protect them. Like Sergeant Bott, he was lost in the forest in my country during the early years of the war that was about to engulf us.

Twenty meters from the clearing in which we stood, in the direction opposite the one from which we had come, a seasonal road ground along to meet the paved highway. Now a deuce-and-a-half rumbled up and stopped at a point in the road closest to where Sergeants Stone and Donaldson and I had been talking. The driver, a boy, was alone in the cab. I did not know him and could not see his shoulder patch.

"I'd like to know what unit he's from," Sergeant Donaldson said, as though he had seen into my mind. "I'd like to know whether he's one of those responsible for choking me."

Captain Dain, a tall, slender, mustachioed officer, stood in the open bed of the truck. "Well," he said, "I have good news and bad news, as the joke goes. Colonel Simons was very pleased with your escape, by the way. No other team has managed that. He was really quite tickled. But—and here's the bad news—you're all under administrative arrest. So to speak. You have to go through the prisoner-of-war camp. The good news is that you'll be fed. So get in the truck and we'll get this show on the road. Lopez!"

"Sir!"

"Give me your knife."

Everybody laughed, both because the captain had anticipated us, which we appreciated, and because our mood had improved with being told that we had pleased the colonel.

The prisoner-of-war camp was located in a disused ammunition bunker. Barbed wire had been stretched in front of the entrance and a guard post established at the gate. The deuce-and-a-half stopped at the guard post and Captain Dain jumped to the ground from the cab. He looked up at us. "Be good now." To the guards, he said, "Watch out for these guys," and then he disappeared into the bunker.

Other guards came out of the bunker and told us to dismount. When the last of us had climbed down out of the truck bed, it pulled away. One by one, we were ordered to take off our clothes and were asked our name, rank, and service number by a man who wrote our answers on a sheet of lined paper fixed to a clipboard. His uniform was barren of nametape, insignia, and symbol of rank. While we were questioned, we were required to bend forward and spread our buttocks with our hands so a guard could inspect our anuses. Master Sergeant Stone went first and I could see the humiliation on his face. By the time it was Sergeant Donaldson's turn, he had so distanced himself that neither humiliation nor any other emotion showed on his face. As for me, modesty takes forms other than the fear of being physically exposed in public.

I did not have an American service number and this caused some confusion when I told our interrogator that I could not provide him one. When I saw the guards' incomprehension and the anger that resulted from this, I informed them that I was an alien and, therefore, had not been assigned one of their numbers. This only added to their dismay and I thought for a moment that one of them would grow angry enough to strike me. But then the man with the clipboard said, "Let it go. We'll take care of it inside."

When everyone was naked and had been questioned, we were marched into the concrete catacomb that was our prison.

Ammunition storerooms had been turned into cells, and in one of these the entire team was shut up. Although we were in a windowless room, enough electrical lighting had been installed as to make it seem midday, no matter what the time; not a single shadow could be seen in our cell, so evenly did the light cover us.

Loudspeakers had been installed in the corridors and they emitted an eerie shriek. I associated this sound with the screams of bats, or perhaps another kind of rodent. The sound coming through the speakers was not always at the same high decibel level; sometimes the volume was lower and occasionally it was turned off altogether. Occasionally, when the volume was low, we heard the screams of men, as though from fear or pain. But this lasted only thirty seconds or even less, and then the shrieking started again. I could not think through it. I would begin a thought but would not be able to sustain the concentration necessary to complete it. Nor could we talk through it, but had to shout to make ourselves heard, so when the volume was turned down we were caught shouting to each other and then the guards blasted us with water from a fire hose, though it was not of such force as to knock any of us over.

Sergeant Donaldson was taken for interrogation. When he returned he was wearing his pants. Everybody else on our team was still naked. In his absence we had been given an aluminum bowl filled with scraps of raw vegetables. It was a kind of salad, but one made from the organic refuse that could be found discarded in a bin behind a mess hall or a produce market. We had saved some for him. Because our dinner had been interrupted by a spraying from the fire hose, the bits of root and leaf that remained floated in a small, silvery pool of water.

"Eat it!" Master Sergeant Stone shouted through the noise from the loudspeaker. "It's all there is!"

Sergeant Donaldson ate some lettuce. He sat down between Master Sergeant Stone and me and shouted: "They told me to wear my pants! Do you think I should take them off?"

Master Sergeant Stone shook his head. "We might be able to use them for something later! If they see that you're not wearing them, they might take them away! I'll explain it to the others!"

Sergeant Donaldson seemed satisfied. It was important that the other soldiers know that he had not broken faith. It was part of our training that prisoners do not break faith with one another. Master Sergeant Stone would assure the others on the team now.

The noise stopped and a guard called for Specialist Larosa. This soldier stood up and another guard motioned him to the barred door, which the guards then opened. Specialist Larosa stepped outside the cell and they took him away after closing and locking the door again.

"What's it like?" Master Sergeant Stone whispered.

Sergeant Donaldson selected his words carefully. When he spoke I could see that he was doing so with consideration for brevity and clarity. He avoided using contractions.

"It was not bad. Just talk. No torture. Just talk. Name.

Rank. Service number. They try to get you to say more. But they only talk. No beating. But they have your Two-oh-one File. And other information. But it is just talk."

The other team members, who had slid closer to Sergeant Donaldson in order to hear him, appeared relieved.

Sergeant Donaldson said: "They make you stare into a light. A high-intensity lamp. There are two men in civilian clothes in front of you and two men in uniform behind you. The ones behind you have weapons. The civilians ask the questions. They try to make you doubt yourself. They belittle you. But it's not too bad." He said the last sentence again with a small modification: "It is not too bad."

"What kind of uniform?" Master Sergeant Stone asked.

"U.S. army."

"What kind of weapons?"

"M-fourteens."

Sergeant Donaldson sat back against the wall and closed his eyes. The part about the light and the number of armed soldiers at his interrogation interested me. I was certain that the thoughtfulness on Master Sergeant Stone's face was inspired by the same disclosure, and not only the disclosure but also the fact that it came almost as an afterthought, as though Sergeant Donaldson considered such details of his interrogation of minor significance. And what did he mean by saying his interrogators tried to make him doubt himself? But I did not have the opportunity to ask him this question or any other, for in a moment we were distracted by Specialist Larosa's return.

"They couldn't figure out if I'm Italian or Mexican. One of them called me a wop and the other called me a spic," he reported.

We all laughed.

Soon Master Sergeant Stone was taken for his interrogation, and after him, Corporal Cobb. While Master Sergeant Stone was away, the guards turned the hose on us again. Some of us, led by Sergeant Donaldson, pretended to enjoy the spraying and washed ourselves, although without soap, as if we were under the stream from a shower.

By mid-evening, everybody on the team had been interrogated. In my own case, I was again asked my name, rank and service number. Again I protested that I did not have an American service number. This time my interlocutors accepted my response at face value and I was escorted back to the cell without further questioning.

Except for me, everybody on our team had been treated similarly. However, some, on their way to the interrogation room or returning from it, had seen men from other teams chained to the grilles of cell doors or being dragged out of the bunker. At the beginning of our captivity we assumed that the guards were making the sounds associated with pain and terror in order to lend to the atmosphere of a prisoner-of-war camp. But now we wondered how severely some men were treated.

Suddenly the bat noise stopped. This was followed by the lights going out. We pressed our backs to the wall and waited to see what would happen next. Soon someone unlocked and opened the door of our cell and threw a bundle inside. He closed the door, but did not lock it, and left.

The bundle was our clothing. Quickly we dressed. We walked out the door single-file. Someone was up ahead of us, standing alone in the dim gray light that issued from a place I could not determine. Master Sergeant Stone went forward and conferred with this man, returning a moment later to tell us, "He's our agent."

"I hope he's better than the last one," Corporal Cobb said, so quietly he almost did not say it.

The agent led us to the rear of the bunker. Here there was an iron gate. The agent pulled on it and it swung open soundlessly. We walked past him into moonlight. We crossed some railroad tracks and then we were in the jungle.

VIII

My feet pointed toward the brown grass of the drop zone. Then the wash from the propeller on the airplane's starboard engine caught me and turned my body, and my boots lifted. Below them now was the soft blue and white of sky and cloud. The line of the horizon canted to the left, then to the right, and now beneath my legs was the deep, succulent green of jungle canopy. My legs whipsawed when the shock of my parachute's inflating hit me.

I drifted along the axis of the drop zone. I could hear the dual sounds of my breathing and my blood pounding. For a few seconds, I could relax and float. I prepared my body to land.

There was a dry canal at the edge of the drop zone and I ran toward it, my rucksack bouncing against my hips. By the time I reached the canal I was close to collapse. I jumped in, turned north and continued on to where the others were resting against its banks. One soldier had passed out from the heat and was being revived by his comrades when I arrived. We had just participated in a demonstration parachute

jump for some Very Important Persons who had flown down
from the United States, one of whom was the next younger
brother of the recently assassinated president.

"Who is she?" Sergeant Jaspers asked.

"She works here," Sergeant Hibbard said.

Sergeants Donaldson, Jaspers, and Hibbard and I were
drinking coffee at a table in the snack bar. Except for Post
Headquarters and the Bachelor Officers Quarters, the snack
bar was the only air-conditioned building on post. Particularly after a parachute jump, when the jumpers wanted to
talk and the NCO club had not yet opened for the evening,
the snack bar was filled with soldiers shouting over one another to tell their stories of the jump and of others it called
to mind. Sergeant Jaspers had asked about the young woman
working the cash register. Her looks and carriage were those
of a North American.

"I mean who's paying her rice bill?" Sergeant Jaspers said.
"Oops. Sorry, sir," he said then, acknowledging the implied
insult. "You're so quiet, I forget you're here."

I nodded, not wishing to worsen a situation that was
merely uncomfortable, nor wanting to believe that Sergeant
Jaspers harbored any malice toward me.

"Watch it, Nick. She's the colonel's daughter," said Sergeant Donaldson.

"My ass," Sergeant Jaspers said.

"Jacobs pays her rice bill," Sergeant Hibbard said as
though I were not sitting beside him.

"Ah, well. Hey, Hibbard, what happened on your lift?
Somebody said something about Brunell getting hurt."

"What's this? What happened?" Sergeant Donaldson said.

"Well, we were jumping equipment—rucksacks and rifles—"

"We all were," said Sergeant Jaspers.

"Every damn jump story has to start with 'We were jumping equipment' or 'We were jumping a C-forty-seven.' As if everybody else was doing something different," said Sergeant Donaldson.

"Hey! You wanna hear this story, shut the fuck up! Read me?"

"Five-by," Sergeant Jaspers said.

"So we were jumping equipment. Brunell was the first man in the stick. Brunell, Chambers, Ruiz, then me. Other guys behind me. Basil jumpmastering. Basil tells Brunell to stand in the door. Brunell makes his pivot, his ruck bounces up off his knees just a little, just enough, the wind catches it and sucks him out. This is what Brunell said later, how it happened. I didn't see it. Anyway, Brunell goes and everybody behind him follows him out. Herd instinct."

"How did he get stuck to the airplane? I heard he got stuck up against the fuselage."

"Yeah, well. I don't know how he did it. I didn't see it. Prop wash probably. C-forty-seven: it can happen. All I know is he was the first man out the door and the last man to land. And the only man who didn't make the DZ."

"He didn't make the DZ?"

"Uh uh. Landed in an ant tree. Fire ants. Bit the hell out of him."

"Jesus," Sergeant Donaldson said. "I got bit on the dick once by fire ants. Made it swell up so much I had to bend over to keep it from rubbing against my pants."

Sergeant Hibbard continued without looking at Sergeant Donaldson. "The best part is that he tried to crawl back inside the airplane. This was when he was plastered against the fuselage, not when he was in the ant tree—I know what you were going to say, Jaspers. He sort of edged himself along the side of the plane until he could get a hand inside the door. Can you imagine seeing everybody jumping past you, the static lines whipping by your face, and you crawling an inch at a time on your belly back to Mother Basil? I heard both Chambers and Ruiz yell something as they went out, but I didn't know what it was until later. They were yelling 'Brunell!'" Sergeant Hibbard mimicked the effect of sound falling away so that the name came out as "Brune-l-l-l!"

"Anyway, Brunell finally manages to get a hand inside the door, but Basil sees it, and what do you think he does? I mean, what would you do? Here's this human hand coming into the airplane from outside. This is not supposed to happen! And Basil, being Basil, decides that this *will* not happen! He stomps on that hand and kicks it and grinds it into the floor of the aircraft! It was all Brunell could do to escape with all his fingers. He finally got himself under the plane and fell free."

"And landed in an ant tree."

"By the time we got him out of the ant tree he was in shock from the ants biting him. He did not look good. His hand looked kind of bad too."

Sergeant Jaspers and Sergeant Donaldson were laughing such that they were on the edge of falling out of their chairs.

"Jesus, that's a great story," Sergeant Donaldson said. "Is it true?"

"I don't know. Everybody tells a part of what seems to be the same story. Brunell, Ruiz, Chambers, Basil—they all seem to confirm it. It is a good one."

"Brunell is in the hospital?"

"Yeah. He's all right. He'll live."

"Well," Sergeant Jaspers said, "there's jungle, danger, and excitement, but no romance. Donaldson wants romance. Right, Paul?"

"What are you talking about?" Sergeant Donaldson said.

"Isn't that what you told me? You like the jungle because of its romance? Didn't you tell me that some native girl bit your dick?"

"How'd we get from jump stories to cock stories?" Sergeant Hibbard said. "Besides, it was Lawrence who told us that story. He said when he was in San Felipe he was swimming in the river with this girl who dived down and bit his dick. She thought it was funny, but it scared the shit out of him. He thought it was a shark or something—*el monstruo.*"

I watched Sergeant Donaldson closely. If he was troubled, he allowed no sign of this to show on his face. All I could detect was what seemed to be disinterest. Perhaps Sergeant Lawrence's first disclosure of the incident with Elena inoculated him against jealousy, or at least precluded any show of pain or outrage. "I only get bit by ants. It's Lawrence who gets bit by girls," he said.

"I'm getting horny," Sergeant Jaspers said. "What's *el monstruo?*"

"Nothing you could fuck," Sergeant Donaldson said.

"Don't count on that, boy."

"It's something in the river that occasionally snatches a

kid off the bank. It's probably an anaconda. It got a little girl a few days before I went there last year," Sergeant Hibbard said.

"Or it could be a shark," Sergeant Donaldson said. "They come into the river at high tide."

"It could be, but you don't see kids on the river bank during high tide. They go out there to wash clothes when the tide is out."

"Yeah, that's true."

"It doesn't sound romantic," Sergeant Jaspers said. "I think you guys just like dick-biters, whatever they are. Me, I want to see naked women dancing by the fire. That's romance. If San Felipe doesn't have that, I'll take Colón. At least the girls there don't bite."

"Only because they can't," Sergeant Hibbard said. He and Sergeant Donaldson laughed. The story told among the young NCOs was that Sergeant Jaspers' girlfriend had been a prostitute on the streets before he began keeping her. She had not been popular until an older woman told her that *yanquis* did not like gold teeth and she had her upper incisors pulled. When her gums healed, she became very popular with *yanquis* and soon she met Sergeant Jaspers.

"Wise guys," Sergeant Jaspers said. "I had her in the ass last night. She said she was letting me fuck her in the ass only because she loves me."

"Does she dance by the fire?" Sergeant Donaldson asked.

"No, she doesn't dance by the fire. I wish she did." Sergeant Jaspers stood up. "I've got to go. I have things to do, people to see. I'm a young sergeant on the way up."

"Braunie is fucking his girl," Sergeant Hibbard said when

Sergeant Jaspers had gone.

Sergeant Donaldson's shoulders moved in a shrug, as if to say it did not matter to him. "Did you meet Kennedy's brother?" I found it interesting that Americans referred to the assassinated president's brother as simply that, the president's brother, as if his identity depended entirely on his relationship with the dead president.

"Yesterday? Yeah. I was one of about seventy-five."

"What did he say?"

"Not much. He wanted to know if we thought we would be able to win if we went to war in Viet Nam. That was all. He thanked us for answering his questions."

"How come only you guys got to meet him?"

"We had all been in either Laos or Viet Nam."

"Oh. He didn't give you a pep talk then? No thank-you's for the loyalty you showed his brother?"

"I think the thanks was implied. But no pep talk."

"What did you tell him?"

"Aren't you full of questions today. You mean about winning? We said we could. What would you expect soldiers to say? 'No, sir, we'll give it our all and we'll lose'?"

"So you tell the president's brother, 'Yes, we'll win, but you shouldn't believe what we say.'"

"Something like that."

"But he doesn't hear the second part, because you don't say it. All he hears is 'Yes, we'll win.' And that's what he takes home with him."

"That's right. Don't look so discouraged, young sergeant. Listen to me. You keep saying 'you' this and 'you' that. 'You said.' 'You told the president's brother.' I want you to know something: you're in it too, babe. Even if you weren't in the

theater with us yesterday, you should be thinking in terms of
we. None of this you-do-that-but-I-do-this shit. It's *we*. It's
always *we*. You got to keep the faith, babe."

"You misled the president's brother."

"*We*, babe. *We*. And we didn't mislead him. We answered
his questions as good soldiers should. Besides, who knows?
Maybe we will win."

Sergeant Donaldson looked at his friend. I did not understand the emotion I saw on his face. Then it went away
and was replaced by resignation. "I'm going to catch the bus
into town. Do you want to go?" he said to Sergeant Hibbard.

And as if they had not just had their discussion, or perhaps because they had had it, Sergeant Hibbard said, "Sure.
Maybe I can talk somebody into lighting a fire and dancing around it. How about you, Lieutenant? Are you up for
town?"

I declined. I wanted to separate myself from these American soldiers, if only for the evening. Viet Nam was my true
home and I had listened to these men move from discussing
the possibility of a new war there to an understanding that
there would indeed be another war. As young as I was, and
as insignificant as I knew these men to be in the hierarchy of
their society, I knew that I had just heard a conversation of
historic moment.

IX

'Chuted up, I lowered myself to a sitting position at the edge
of the runway. The night was heavy with humidity and my
shirt was already soaked through with sweat. I took my hel-

met off and set it beside my leg.

"Has everybody been inspected! Anybody not been in-spected!"

I put my helmet back on and levered myself to my feet. I waddled over to where Master Sergeant Stone was shouting for men to get their equipment checked for the jump.

"You been inspected, sir?"

"No, Master Sergeant."

Master Sergeant Stone smiled at my odd way of address-ing him. In the American army, NCOs, regardless of senior-ity, were addressed as Sergeant or Sarge, but as long as I had served with Americans, I had not been able to force myself to address a master sergeant as "Sarge." To my ears, it sound-ed disrespectful, a failure to acknowledge accomplishment. (Rereading this passage, I see that I am mistaken: there was the occasion in the forest when we were waiting for the truck to take us to the prisoner-of-war camp—I addressed Master Sergeant Stone as "Sergeant" then, but I had meant it as a term of disrespect. But that was a single occasion and it oc-curred during what seemed like another era as we stood on the runway, preparing for the jump.)

Master Sergeant Stone's hands moved over my jump gear. His fingers snapped elastic bands and tugged on metal con-nectors. Finally he handed my static line to me over my right shoulder. I fastened it to the carrying handle of my reserve parachute. I returned to the verge of the runway and sat down. Soon I had to urinate and I got to my feet again and went to where the forest began with high grass and clumps of uncut brush. I found myself standing beside Sergeant Hibbard who was already peeing.

"How ya doin', Lieutenant?"

"Hello, Sergeant."

"You got your orders, huh?"

"Yes."

"When do you go?"

"Next month."

"So soon? I didn't think it would be this quick. Are you anxious to see your home again?"

"Yes. I have been gone for a long time. Several years."

"Oh? Were you somewhere else before you joined us? In the army, I mean."

"Yes."

I did not elaborate only because I did not want to think about returning home. I was not certain any longer where my home was and this new knowledge of myself disquieted me. When one is homesick, the memory of one's home, the sense of security it represents, is comforting. But now, faced with actually going home, possibly to stay for the rest of my life, I remembered the rooms of the house I had grown up in and I remembered my mother and saw her face again in the heat of argument and I felt suffocated, as though my life were ending. I finished urinating and went back to the runway and found a place to sit down apart from the other jumpers.

In a moment, everybody was called to a spot thirty meters or so behind the aircraft for the briefing. A bespectacled captain stood in front of an easel on which were his charts. Nobody could see what was on them. All anybody could see, except perhaps for the soldiers who sat on the ground closest to the easel, was that they were made of white paper. At intervals the captain flipped a chart over to reveal another chart that was as white as the previous one. Sometimes he slapped one with his pointer. When he did this, a noise came from it like a firecracker exploding.

"Blah blah blah," the captain said. "I'm Captain blah blah, the Marshalling Area Control blah. Blah blah blah blah twenty-three hundred hours. Blah blah blah twelve hundred fifty feet. Blah blah DZ blah blah personnel and equipment bag blah blah rucksack blah blah blah no moon blah stars blah light blah so okay. Boats blah sharpshooters blah blah French Canal blah blah Chagres River blah blah blah just in case sharks blah you land in water blah blah. That's all."

I found the other men in my stick and sat down with them.

"I don't see any stars," the soldier beside me said. I recognized him as B Company's supply sergeant. "It's cloudy. There's no stars."

The next man down said, "It's supposed to clear by twenty-three hundred. That's what the MACO said."

"Bullshit. It's not going to clear in the next hour. And even if we had stars, we wouldn't have any light. Stars don't give light. The moon gives light. And there's no moon tonight."

"Look. What's the difference. You're going to jump anyway. It doesn't matter if it's raining or snowing or the jungle's on fire. If they tell you to jump, you're going to jump. Right? So quit your bitching."

After a while, the supply sergeant said, "Fuckin' shark boats, for all the good they do."

My skin hurt. It ached. I did not know why. It had hurt all day, as though the nerve endings had somehow moved too close to the surface. Even the breeze whiskering across it left it throbbing. Also, my uniform seemed not to fit as it usually did, but hung on me as though it had been made for another, larger man. My skin felt as though it were being abraded by the material, with its unusual roughness and its seemingly heavier weight. Rigging my equipment, the big PAE bag and my rucksack and rifle, and then 'chuting up and getting inspected and attending the MACO briefing, I had not had time to think about my skin's having become so sensitive. But now it occurred to me that the entire day had been… awkward, as though something was awry in its very fabric.

The red lights came on on the wings of the aircraft and also inside. I could see their glow inside past the lowered tail ramp. It came to me then that something bad was going to happen. At first I thought it was only the play of the red light on the men's faces that made the day seem so spooky, but then I knew that there was something bad in the day itself. I began to consider my body's sensations and sought to determine whether the space between myself and any of the other men was somehow distorted—"as though looking at them through water," Sergeant Hibbard had said—but did not find a distortion. Then I looked for the sensation of cold that might be issuing from one of the others—"like someone had left a freezer door open"—but I did not find that either. Then, in a flash, I was struck by a fragment of a thought that told me that the others were in no danger at all, but before I could locate the rest of the thought I told myself that I should rehearse the jump in my mind; I should make certain I understood the procedure because we did not jump the PAE bag very often.

I would go out the jump door and two or three seconds later my canopy would inflate. I had better assume that my risers would be twisted. The prop wash will catch the PAE bag and turn me and that will twist the risers. Very good. Then I kick my legs until the risers untwist and in a moment I am floating, checking my canopy, no suspension lines looped over it, my rate of descent—I compare my rate of descent with that of the other jumpers and I am fine, I am coming down fine, I see that my rate of descent is no faster than the others'. I am coming down and I am in no danger of colliding with another jumper and here are the trees, I am at what is called "treetop level" and I pull on the two quick releases attached to my D rings and the PAE bag drops away and stops short thirty feet below me because it is tied with nylon rope to my parachute harness and it hangs there below me until it hits the ground, I will feel it, the sudden easing of its weight pulling me down, and now I have only a second or two between the bag's hitting the ground and my own landing which will not be pleasant because I will be riding my rucksack in and it will be pressing between my knees so that I will not be able to keep my feet together and, clearly, I am going to land like a sack of shit, as they say. So everything is fine. I am on the ground and I am not dead and in my mind everything is fine.

Master Sergeant Stone was passing the word to load up. I got to my feet. I followed the supply sergeant up the ramp into the airplane. I sat down in one of the inboard seats and passed the seat belt under my reserve parachute and buckled it by feel. When we were in the air, I asked the supply sergeant, "Are you afraid?" The supply sergeant nodded his head. But I knew he was afraid only in the ordinary way. It was the fear everybody felt before a jump. I knew, too, that what I was experiencing was not ordinary.

The plane would make two passes over the drop zone. Outboard personnel, those seated against the skin of the aircraft, would jump on the first pass, those in the inboard seats on the second. The outboard personnel had already hooked up to the static line cable when I heard the voice. It said in my native language: "It's you! You are the one!" (I remember that I was surprised that it did not speak to me in English.) It left no opportunity for denial or refusal. It simply informed me of the nature of things. I was certain that no one else had heard the voice because, as loud as it was, it had come from inside my head and I was sure it had not carried beyond the lining of my skull. Still, I looked around at the other men. Apprehension was on everyone's face, but it was nothing compared to what I felt.

The outboard personnel had gone. Master Sergeant Stone gave the command for inboard personnel to stand up. Everybody stood. We hooked up our static lines even before the command came to do it. For a fraction of a second before the command to check equipment was given, I felt something intrude in the routine. It was as though something had altered in the cosmos. It was a moment's distraction, nothing more, and immediately it was gone. Then I wanted nothing so much as to jump out of the airplane.

The remainder of the jump commands came quickly. My adrenalin kicked in and I was shuffling to the door. Master Sergeant Stone was screaming as we raced out of the aircraft: "Go! Go! Go! Get out of my airplane! Go!"

I felt my body begin a slow spin. Then my canopy opened. I could not raise my head—my risers were twisted down to the back of my neck. I began a bicycling motion with my legs and in a couple of seconds or less the risers were freed and I looked up and checked my canopy for holes or malfunctions. The canopy was fine and I looked around for other jumpers so I could compare my rate of descent with theirs, but I did not see any others.

My hands ran down past my reserve to check my equipment. Something was wrong. What? My rucksack was gone. Where it should have been, I could touch my pelvis. Again I had the sense that the day was somehow out of balance, but it was not so much a feeling now as an acknowledgment.

Now, against the two darknesses of sky and earth, I picked out the deeper darkness of the forest and saw it was time to drop the PAE bag. My fingers found the quick releases, hesitated, and then pulled. I felt the bag hit the end of the rope. It was good not to have its weight against my legs any longer.

And now, sailing across the skyscape at the same altitude I was, came another jumper. The darkness of the jungle was behind him and his canopy ballooned against the darkness of the heavens. Rushing at each other, neither he nor I spoke. Neither of us attempted to move out of the other's way, but each allowed his parachute to carry him directly into the course of the other. At last I pulled hard on my right riser, seeing, as I pulled, the other man doing the same, and each of us, as though dancers in a choreographed performance, began a counterclockwise movement in a parabolic arc around the other. Now I felt a tug at my harness and recognized it as the weight of the PAE bag. I saw the trunks of trees stabbing frantically at the sky. I had no time to ready myself to land and I came down with all of my weight on my left foot. I heard the *Crack!* of my leg breaking and felt the pain instantly. It was so intense that I could not scream.

It was deeper than I had breath for.

I lay on my side, my left leg covering my right. My canopy filled with the night breeze and began to drag me. I released the capewell on my left shoulder and my riser sprang away from it. My body relaxed again. I saw now, not twenty feet away, another jumper. He was stuffing his parachute into his kit bag. He had to be the same jumper with whom I had nearly collided; no one else could have landed so close to me.

"Sir!" I shouted. "Sir? I need help, please."

The other man swung his kit bag onto his back. He replaced his helmet on his head and walked away.

After awhile I shouted: "Medic!"

"Sometime during the jump commands the thought occurred to me that I did not have to jump. I did not have to go out of the airplane just because Master Sergeant Stone was telling me to go. But by then it was too late; I was determined."

"Herd instinct," Sergeant Hibbard said.

"It felt like...fulfillment. I would do what was expected. And if I died, well... I thought I was going to die."

"I don't know, sir. If I heard a voice telling me not to jump, I think I would give some heavy consideration to not jumping."

"It did not tell me not to jump. It told me only that something was going to happen to me. It did not tell me that I could do anything about it. I thought I was going to die."

Sergeant Hibbard, Sergeant Donaldson and I were sitting in the snack bar at a table against the wall. My left leg, in a cast, was propped on a chair. I could not stop talking.

"When we were standing outside the airplane I felt that something was wrong. I looked for that coldness that you said comes from some men who are going to die. I also looked for the distortion of space between myself and any of the others that you said may sometimes happen. But I didn't see feel coldness or see a distortion."

Sergeants Hibbard and Donaldson were looking at each other. Sergeant Hibbard turned to me. "I said all that?"

"I'm sure you did."

"I don't think so."

"An American who has been in Viet Nam told me those things. I'm certain it was you."

"I don't think so, sir. But I'll tell you something. I don't think you should be talking about things like that. You talk about things, sometimes you make them happen."

"I thought you told me."

"No."

"Well," I said. "Anyway." I was embarrassed. I remained convinced that Sergeant Hibbard had told me those things, but I felt I had been caught crossing a border, although one that was unmarked. Sergeant Donaldson, occasionally the diplomat, rescued me.

"So which bone is it? The big one or the little one?"

"The little one. The fibula."

"At least it's not the big one. It would be worse then."

"Yes. It's a spiral fracture. The doctor called it a paratrooper's injury. He said it was very common among paratroopers."

Sergeant Hibbard shook his head. He took my cup and Sergeant Donaldson's and his own and went over to the coffee urn and refilled them. When he returned to the table, he said, "You never found out who the guy was you almost crashed into?"

"No. But I'm certain he was the same person who left me on the drop zone."

"Well, one good thing is that you get to stay in this country a while longer. Or will they make you go anyway?"

Sergeant Hibbard had gotten the idea from someone that the government of my country was trying to coerce me to return to my homeland. This was not true. I had not been asked to return. Had I been asked, I would have done so without resistance. Sergeant Hibbard and I had discussed this matter before and I had been unable to convince him that I had nothing against my country's government. For me, my country was its people—*my* people, my family and those closest to my family—and the nature of our government, as long as it did not bring calamity to us, was of little importance. But Sergeant Hibbard apparently was not able to conceive of a person who, at the same time, could be loyal to his own country and to the army of a nation that found itself in an increasingly disputatious relationship with his natal land. I had given up trying to disabuse him, having come to think that Sergeant Hibbard needed to believe that the world could be approached simply and directly, if only one were simple and direct. But he was staring at me, waiting for my response, and I said, "They won't make me go," and hoped that that would suffice.

"I could live in this country forever," Sergeant Donaldson said. "But I'm set to leave. I've said my goodbyes."

"It isn't fun," said Sergeant Hibbard. He was alluding to his experience in Viet Nam.

"You want to go back. You told me you do."

"Yeah. But it isn't fun. It's fine for me, but I wouldn't recommend it to anyone else. Do you think you'll find what you're looking for there?"

"I don't know," Sergeant Donaldson said. "What am I looking for?"

"I don't know, babe. I thought you knew. What about you, Lieutenant? Do you think you'll find what you're looking for someday?"

"I am not looking for anything, Sergeant. I wish only to pass my life—" I could not think of the word which would most accurately convey what I wanted to say. Instead, I used the word "profitably."

Of course the Americans laughed, believing I meant profit in terms of capital. I let it go. I had grown tired of playing the alien playing the American.

Later in my life, I would experience again the kind of anxiety, if that is what it was, that made my skin feel raw, as if it had been freshly abraded, and which was accompanied by the sense that my clothing was awry on my body, but I never heard that voice of warning again. These feelings occurred only when I was about to engage in something potentially perilous, and then only sometimes. When I paid attention to them, I was able to avoid harm. When I did not, I paid for my heedlessness.

X

In the following weeks, Sergeant Donaldson vanished from the Isthmus of Panama, having been reassigned to my coun-

try. I would never see him again, although once, in Viet
Nam, I thought I saw him through my binoculars—there
was something about the gait of the soldier I was watching
that reminded me of him—but I could not be sure and soon
became convinced that I was deluding myself.

I passed much of my time in my quarters or the snack
bar. I felt uncomfortable in the Officers Club, for my association with NCOs, coupled with my foreignness, made
me doubly suspect in the eyes of the officers, and the NCO
Club no longer welcomed me since the departure not only
of Sergeant Donaldson but also of so many other NCOs I
had known. Without Sergeant Donaldson's companionship,
Sergeant Hibbard no longer sought my company. In any
event, he soon received his own orders assigning him to Viet
Nam and shortly afterward he himself disappeared.

Events in my own country during this time became wor-
risome. My only source of information was my mother's letters. My mother was a perceptive woman and I trusted the
veracity of the information in her letters, but her world was
bounded by the activities of our family and neighbors, and
I had developed a hunger for the larger world. Still, as my
family was involved, however peripherally, in the fortunes of
our country, news of either implied news of the other.

My uncle's business in exports had expanded. He now
had agents throughout the Peninsula who bought ceramic
goods and historical artifacts, when they could locate them,
for resale to European and American importers. My sister
had graduated from university. Having learned several European languages, she was doing well in our uncle's employ.
My mother suggested in her letters that perhaps it was time
for me to return home and take a position beside my sister.

With my knowledge of the Americans, I would be of great value to my uncle, and so on.

My other uncle, who also worked for his older brother, had been killed in an ambush on our western border. My mother did not say, perhaps did not know, who ambushed his party. I surmised that it could have been government soldiers—our government—or possibly soldiers of the government of our western neighbor or bandits acting on their own or hired by one of my surviving uncle's competitors. What was his brother doing so far west? My mother did not address this question, but I guessed that he was smuggling certain items into our country, certain items being quantities of gold or gems or opium, perhaps without elder brother's knowledge. I remembered my mother's younger brother as being of a reckless sort, and impulsive.

There had been another coup, made by an alliance of generals from our army and air force. The coup was successful in that they had replaced the president. It was unsuccessful in that the generals were now not able to decide who among them should be supreme.

I received a letter from my mentor, an officer of high rank who had enabled me to attend my initial officer training, and thus to obtain my commission. He enjoined me not to return home. He was in disfavor now and was not certain how tenable his position was. Should he fall, those whose careers he had promoted would likewise be in peril of losing everything, including, perhaps, their lives. As a patriot, I wanted to return to my country to participate in the resistance, but as his protégé I did not want to act without his approval. I was surprised by the emotion I felt upon learning of my mentor's difficulties. It was not something I had experienced before. Although I labeled it patriotism, I think now it is more accurately characterized as love for this man who had been my guide during the most difficult time with my parents and whom I now desired to protect. But perhaps that is patriotism. Perhaps patriotism begins with the love for a single person.

In any case, there was no resistance that either I or my mentor, who was better situated than I to determine the existence of such a political movement, could discern. Shortly after I informed him that I would remain with the American army if our government and the American government agreed, or, failing this, I would pursue advanced studies at an American university—I did not even declare what subject I wished to study—I received a letter from an office of my government that I had not previously heard of offering me a small stipend to study in the United States. On an attached sheet was a list of American universities that had accepted students from my country in the past.

Ten days later I received a second letter, this one from the Office of the Chief of the Army, inviting me to resign my commission. A form was attached which only awaited my signature to abrogate the results of the commissioning ceremony of a few years earlier. I suspected there would be unforeseen consequences—unforeseen by me, anyway—if I signed the form, and I wrote my mentor, asking his advice. He did not respond. Many years later, over after-dinner coffee, I asked him about the meaning of the army's letter and his failure to reply to mine. He had not heard of the former and had never received the latter. But, he said, had he received my letter, he would have advised me to leave the army, or at least to delay responding to the army's letter. It was a terrible time, not only for soldiers, but for every class of person in our country, and there were no signposts on any road one might choose to take.

I did not sign the form and did not return it. Nor did I respond to the accompanying letter. I never heard any more about either.

From the list of universities my government had provided me, I selected four that I had heard of or were located in an area of the United States that I thought would be interesting to live in for a short time. I say "a short time" because during that period of my life I could not imagine myself more than two or three years older. I assumed that no matter where I was or what I was doing, I would be somewhere else, doing something different, in twenty-four or thirty-six months.

I must now acquaint you with a severe change in my life that would make for other, even more extreme changes. Probably out of loneliness, for my friends had left and the discomfort in my leg prevented my even walking to Post Headquarters to find some work I could do, I had begun seeing a woman with some frequency. I cannot say that I found her particularly desirable, at least at first, but I was able to talk to her as I had no other American. Yes, she was American, at least by citizenship. It was not long before I realized that while I had done a great deal of talking about myself, she had offered very little information about herself. Even knowing this, however, I continued to confide the most intimate aspects of my family's relations with one another, waiting for her to open the floodgates of revelation about her life that would show me who this person was who was becoming so important to me.

I met her through the young Indian woman who cleaned my quarters. I had asked her to bring me a woman who would allow me to make love to her. I made this request out of pique, for she had just rejected my proposal that she become my mistress. Even after I described to her the depths of my loneliness she continued to shake her head with such conviction that I did not repeat my offer.

But two days later she peered into my room as I lay on the bed, reading, and a moment afterward a taller woman of indeterminate nationality walked in. The door closed behind her. As she had not touched it, I assumed that my friend had made me a gift, and her closing the door was her communication of that fact.

The woman wore a green dress with a floral print. Her skin was brown and her hair black. It was cut fashionably close at the neck and ears. It was a white woman's haircut and she carried herself as though she were white. Her face was striking: straight nose with a narrow bridge, eyes so dark I thought they must either lead to infinity or were entirely without depth, a complexion so without flaw that I wanted immediately to rub my cheek against hers. Still, my taste was for small, compact women and I thought I could tell from the flesh of her bare legs that her body would not be firm.

I gestured to her to sit in the chair beside my bed. Her dress was short and rose up her thighs as she sat down. From my position, leaning on one elbow, I could see up her skirt. She allowed her legs to part slightly and I saw the sheen of white underpants against rich brown skin. I inhaled deeply, hoping to catch her aroma, but I was disappointed. She was smiling, as though in spite of herself.

"What's your name?" I asked in Spanish.

She hesitated, then said, "Elena."

I looked at her sharply. "Why did you pick that name?"

"Because it's my name in Spanish," she said in accentless English.

"You're not Panamanian?"

"Yes, I am."

I mentioned earlier that I had once made love with a woman who had lived in New York and who spoke perfect conversational American English, so while I was interested in Elena's history, I was not bemused by the answers she offered to my questions. I asked her to take off her clothes. She did, but with some awkwardness, as though she was not accustomed to being stared at while defenseless. I assumed her to be a prostitute, but her disconcertion was certainly not that of a whore. Her body actually looked quite solid and even comparatively unused. Her breasts and buttocks were heavy and full and as, upon my gesture, she moved toward me, I found myself wanting to stuff these sensual portions of her in my mouth at once, as though they were sweet fruits.

I asked her to help me with my pants. While she pulled them past my cast, I fondled her. By the time she had gotten them off, I was aroused. I patted the mattress in invitation, but did not leave enough room for her to lie down. As she sat, I placed my hand, palm up, beneath her and my fingers went inside her. She did not object. She did not object to anything I did to her that day, though I was determined to humiliate her. I was angry, but I did not understand why. It had to do, I think, with my sense of being isolated, and of being unable to alter the events that were beginning to consume my family and my friends. I say "I think" because even now I am not certain about what stimulated my anger. It is easy, looking back, to combine the affairs of the world with my own uncharitable desires in order to define a cause-and-effect relationship, but who can rely on memory to render the past, especially the emotional past, accurately? For whatever reason, I wanted to see another human being degraded, and I was able to degrade this woman.

When I had finished, I asked her how much she charged. I saw the same hesitation I had observed when earlier I asked her name.

"Twenty dollars?" It came as a question, as though she were not certain of her value.

When I did not immediately respond, her face became wooden and she said, "You don't have to pay me if you don't want to."

I wanted to weep. I was ashamed of what I had done, but even at that moment—and I am sure that on this occasion memory does not betray me—I sensed that she had endured other things, worse things than those I had inflicted.

I asked her to get my wallet from the dresser. I gave her two twenty-dollar bills and asked her to return tomorrow.

"I can't tomorrow," she said.

"The next day then?"

"Yes. The day after tomorrow."

We agreed on the time. Then I asked her, though I could not have said why, "What will you do with the money?"

She smiled but did not offer an answer.

Yet I wanted to know, for almost as soon as she came through the doorway again, I asked, "What did you do with the money I gave you?"

She smiled quizzically, seemed about to answer, and then said instead, "Why do you want to know?"

But I did not reply. Instead, I lay back against my pillows and asked her to undress me.

Her body seemed familiar to me this time, although I knew this was a deception I was foisting on myself. I did not know her body and I did not know her. Still, I recognized her smell and the way her breasts fell when she leaned forward. I wanted to do certain things and again she did not object, though once I thought I saw her face twisted with pain. But when I looked again, her countenance was placid, and a moment later she said she liked what I was doing.

Afterward, as she lay beside me—yes, she lay beside me as I recovered myself, as though it was the most natural thing for her to do—I asked her, "How long have you been a prostitute?"

She looked at me with hostility. "Why do you ask?"

"I am curious. I have no hidden reason for asking."

She relaxed then, and said, "Not long." Then she asked, "Do you think I'm good?"

"Yes, of course."

"'Of course.' I mean do you think I'm good enough to make a lot of money this way?"

"It isn't a question of being good, whatever you mean by that. How much money?"

"I don't know."

I was very sleepy and asked her to leave. I gave her forty dollars and told her I wouldn't be able to afford her until the following week when I would be paid. I asked her to return next Tuesday afternoon.

When, the following day, the maid came in to straighten my room, I asked her about her friend who called herself Elena. She grinned so broadly that I wondered if she would not injure her facial muscles. But she said, "Elena? I don't know someone named Elena."

I did not say anything more. I did not understand the game she wanted to play and, not knowing the rules, I felt I must lose. I pretended to go back to my reading and kept my nose in the book until she left.

When she returned the next day, I asked her to tell me about her friend who might or might not call herself Elena.

She smiled again, though not so earnestly. There was thought behind her smile.

"She is not my friend," she said.

"But you know her well?"

"Yes. But not as a friend."

"As what then?"

"She is my boss."

She smiled again, the smile not so wide as the one the day before, but a good deal wider than the one a few moments earlier. Then she left.

On the day after, I asked her to tell me about her boss who might be called Elena.

"She is not really my boss," she said. She did not bother to smile this time, but added immediately, "Her father is my boss." Then, before I could ask in what way was Elena's father her boss, she asked me, "Do you love her?"

I had no idea what to say. I did not know what she meant by the word "love," or what I might mean should I say it. I asked, "Does she love me?"

She thought for a second or two, then said, "No. Why

would she?"

"I don't know. Why would I love her?" We were speaking matter-of-factly, as in my country farmers might talk about the possibilities of a bountiful rice harvest or of another change in the government. At the same time, we were both careful not to reveal anything that might present the other with an advantage, although, for my part, I did not think I would recognize an advantage were it offered to me, nor comprehend when I had given one. We were playing a mysterious game with arcane rules, and I was only beginning to realize that I was losing.

But she did answer my last question. "You would love her because she is so beautiful. And because she does not complain."

"Do you know her so well that you know she does not complain?"

"I see her every day. She tells me everything."

"Everything? I would like to know what kind of boss tells her employee everything."

"I told you, she is not my boss. And she tells me everything. Some of the things you do with her—I would not like that. Why do you do those things?"

"Which things do you mean?"

"You know which things. The ones you do with her body."

"But which things? Which doesn't she like? Or which would you not like?"

She shook her head. She was obviously uncomfortable. "I cannot tell you."

I apologized for embarrassing her, saying, "I did not mean to make you blush. I thought we were enjoying ourselves by teasing each other."

She shook her head again. "I am too young."

I considered asking her age, but I was not certain she
was referring to her age and I did not want to embarrass
her further, so I apologized once more and then picked up a
book as if I was going to read it. She picked up some bits of
newspaper from the floor and put them in the trash basket
and then she emptied the trash basket into a larger container
in the hall. Then she left.

The next day and the day after were the weekend, so I
did not see her. On Monday I was at Post Headquarters,
having taken a taxi to pick up my paycheck, when she came,
so I missed her that day. On Tuesday she did not come, but
Elena did.

"Did you say something to my maid to upset her?" she
asked after I had made love to her. Her back was to me. I
moved my hand over her thigh, luxuriating in the smoothness of her flesh against my palm.

"Your maid?" I was not thinking. I was preoccupied with
the pleasure my senses were bringing to me. I inhaled her
scent.

"Maria. The Kuna girl."

"My maid?"

"Mine, too. Did you say something to her?"

"Your maid?"

She turned to look into my face. "Who did you think
she was?"

"I didn't know." I moved back from her gaze. My own
traveled to her breasts. Her aureoles were very large, deep
brown and almost perfectly circular. I took a nipple between my thumb and forefinger. I could see pleasure replace

thought in her face. "Who are you?" I asked.

"What?"

I laughed and so did she. I took her other nipple in my mouth. Releasing it, I asked again, "Who are you?"

"I don't understand what you mean."

"You're not a whore. Who are you?"

She shook her head but did not say anything.

"I want to know. Who are you?"

"Later. I'll tell you later."

"Who are you?"

"What's the difference? You get what you want. What you pay for."

"Am I the first man who has paid you?"

"So what if you are? What does it matter?"

"Why are you crying?"

"I'm not crying. Oh. I didn't know I was."

"Why are you crying then?"

"Don't you ever give up? Because you ask me these questions. Because I don't want to answer. Haven't I been good to you? Haven't I done what you wanted? Isn't that enough? God!"

She could have got up from the bed at any time. She could have risen and dressed and walked out the door and I could not have stopped her, but she did not. She lay beside me, naked beside my nakedness, and sobbed long, agonized sobs that came from somewhere beneath her chest. I remembered these sounds as having come from someone else, long ago, but I did not remember who had made them, nor on what occasion. (Later that day, lying alone in the dark of dusk settling, the air thickening around me, I did remember. They were the sounds my mother had made during her father's funeral. They were the sounds of grief, of the spirit dying.)

I placed my arm under her head and, grasping her shoulder, pulled her toward me. She came willingly, seeking comfort where she could. Her tears flowed without ceasing even for an instant. I petted her as I would a child and asked her no more questions. I was coming to love her, though I could not have said why. Even so, I knew her physical attractiveness and her sexual pliancy had little to do with the growth of this emotion in me. I know now that I am drawn to women in emotional turmoil. There is a moral quality to their pain that attracts me, just as the moral ambiguity of soldiers' lives continues to fascinate me.

Soon she was asleep. As she slept, I caressed her breasts, lingering at the nipples. I was taken by their length. After ten or fifteen minutes had passed I saw her smile, and then her eyes opened and in a moment she was straddling me. When we were done, we thanked each other. Yes, it is true, we did thank each other, for each of us had recognized in the other a hunger that could not be sated, though we did not share the same hunger and could not even have defined it if challenged to do so, and our final congress that day was a sign that at the deepest level we were beginning to know each other.

I told her that I would like to see her more often, but I could not afford to pay for more frequent visits. She said in turn that she would like to visit me more often also, but needed time to consider the financial aspect of our arrangement. I asked her to return the next day, but she said she could not, that Friday was the soonest she would be able. We agreed on Friday.

I still had not seen past the façade of mystery she presented to me on her visits, except to fathom that she was profoundly unhappy. Who was she? If she was not a whore, then what was she? And, if she was not a whore, then why was she selling herself? Did she want to degrade herself? But why?

I cannot say I formulated these questions so many years ago as I have set them down here. My mind was not as analytical or as disciplined as it became later. Yet, although not clearly put, the questions existed and they gnawed at me like something feral that I harbored within myself. I avoided introspection then. I was young and, like most young people, I sought pleasure or, if pleasure was impossible, then something else that would stimulate me, either in body or mind. If I sought knowledge of the world, I did not yet comprehend that such knowledge must bring its own pain, its particular brand of grief and despair.

On Friday afternoon, soon after Elena and I made love, as she lay quietly in the fold of my arm, the sweat still drying on our bodies—she was pulling, unconsciously, I think, at the sparse hairs on my forearm—she began to talk about herself. She was what in the United States is called a half-breed, what in my country we call a half-caste. Her father was of North American—meaning northern European—extraction and her mother was a mixed-blood from Panama's Pacific coast. After telling me this, perhaps detecting that it made no difference to me, she went on. She and her father were lovers. That was how she expressed it, as if the relationship were voluntary on both their parts. Then she said her father had violated her when she was very small and that he continued to use her even to the present day. She cried again, as she had cried on Tuesday, in agony, and seemed not to be able to hear the words I used in my attempt to soothe her. I held her, feeling that it was only my arms around her that prevented her from disintegrating entirely. After several minutes she quieted, and then she was asleep.

I could not comprehend what I had heard. Rather, I understood what she had said, but I did not appreciate its significance. Recall that my country was again on the lip of war, one of my uncles had been killed, my mentor feared for his life, and I did not know what I should do about any of it or even if I should do anything. Here, in Panama, I had known a woman who, when she was fourteen, was raped by her stepfather while her mother held her down; when she had healed they made her walk the streets. All of this was in my mind as Elena made her confession to me. (Yes, it was a confession, for, although I did not realize it then, she had taken into herself all the secret guilt that belonged to her father—and to her mother, who had known for years the nature of the relationship between her husband and her daughter, perhaps was even her husband's accomplice, as the mother of my former lover was her husband's.) So I did not view Elena's experience as particularly important. To me, at that time, it was simply another ugly aspect of life in the West. I did not see her relationship with her father as providing the explanation for the inconsistencies and contradictions I had begun to observe in her moods and behavior. And I did not understand that one person's experience of life is the same as another's only at the most superficial level. Each of us is alone, but I was only beginning to learn this, for I had not lived long among Americans.

She slept for perhaps half an hour. Even in so short a time, the light in the room had dimmed. My body had cooled so that I would have liked to pull the sheet up over us, but I had let it go in order not to disturb her with my movement. She had been awake for a minute or two before I knew it. I turned my head to look at her and found her staring at me. Her expression was tentative; she was wondering, I assumed, how I would take all that she had told me. I touched her face with my free hand and she began to cry again, although not so without restraint. Then she stopped and I kissed her cheek where it was wet. Soon we were making love again. I was careful to read her body to see what she wanted; I was very careful not to cause her pain. It was not long before she climaxed.

Resting again, I told her I wanted to marry her and asked her if she would like to marry me. I had not intended to propose marriage. I had not thought about marriage to her, or to anyone. Yet these words came out of my mouth, and before I could stop them they were gone. What had possessed me? For it was as if I were indeed possessed by something determined to have its own way, regardless of my intentions. It was willing to allow me the conviction that I could plot my own destiny, knowing full well that what it permitted me was self-delusion.

What was it? Was my loneliness so profound that I would marry a woman I hardly knew and of whom my family would certainly not approve? Was my future so uncertain that I was willing to clasp her body to my own as a kind of anchor? Had my country's and my family's instability so affected me that I needed an anchor just to hold fast the present? Yet, if I am filled with wonder now at the fact of my binding myself to a woman about whom I knew so little, and to a life that I anticipated, even as I lay beside her, would be filled with distress, I know too that, though I had not contemplated marrying her or, for that matter, anything beyond coitus with her, speaking the words of my proposal and hearing her reply brought me a kind of fulfillment. If I was surprised by what I had done, I was not unhappy.

When I imagine her now, I do not have a clear picture of her. I believe I would know her immediately should I somehow be able to see her again as she was then, but I cannot recall her features. I remember aspects of her body. Perhaps I valued her body more than anything else about her. Perhaps that is why I suffered so when I thought about her giving herself to others. I know I said earlier that the growth of my love for her had little to do with her physical beauty, and that is true. But once I acknowledged my love for her, it encompassed her very physicality, the beauty of which drew men to her as though signaling her availability. As my love deepened, it sought to imprison everything about her that was not me, everything about her that I did not understand—or, perhaps, it wanted to imprison everything about her that was also me and that I was beginning to know too well.

I remember how her back indented as it met the flow of her hips, and the fullness of her buttocks, and the smoothness, like liquid satin, of her skin at the inside of her thighs. She moistened quickly (she said I did, too) and experienced orgasms that left her skin so sensitive that she could not bear to be touched anywhere on her body for several minutes afterward. I can recall all of this about her, yet cannot imagine a complete person. Perhaps this is because her personality was not finished when I knew her. Or perhaps it is because she never revealed anything I could grasp as a key to understanding her beyond the fact of her father's using her.

Why did she agree to marry me? Months later, I asked her that question and she said she loved me. I did not believe her. Certainly she wanted to escape her father. Perhaps also she wanted to reverse the course of self-degradation and -destruction she knew she was on. I think this is true and, possibly, if she is still alive, she would agree. But, being young, we pretended for as long as we could that some things did not exist, or did not matter, and so some things went unrecognized.

Her parents lived in a house on a hill cleared of trees overlooking Gatun Lake, the lake that feeds the locks of the canal. Tiles made of rubber or something like rubber covered the floors in a checkered pattern. I learned later—much later, in fact, in one of those conversations with foreign visitors that leave you with an item of information that enhances knowledge of no significance gathered a lifetime before—that this method of covering a floor had been popular in the United States half a century earlier but was no longer in fashion there. Heavy wooden furniture—chairs, tables, couches, a desk—occupied every room. I recognized it as having come from a military warehouse, for the furniture in my room in the Bachelor Officers Quarters was of the same style, wood and finish as these pieces. The sitting room faced west and so, through its many windows, captured the light of the declining sun, making the end of the day the cheeriest part.

Elena's father was a large, sallow-complected man. His face was the color and appeared to be of the consistency of yellowing wax. I tried to picture him giving her pleasure, but found it impossible. (Yet he sometimes did, she told me.) He was an attorney and he dressed in the manner of North American attorneys in Panama: a gray or white linen suit, a white shirt with the collar unbuttoned, black or brown boots of the kind known as "cowboys." When we shook hands upon meeting for the first time, he looked at me in such a way as to remind me of the police in my own country.

Her mother was a tiny woman who seemed to be trying to appear shrewd as she appraised me. I think, though, that there was little, if anything, cunning or calculating about her. Her skin was the color of cocoa and her Indian ancestry could be detected in her prominent cheekbones and ovoid eyes. She echoed her husband's opinions on everything except racial matters. I would have thought that she had never enjoyed a life independent of her husband's, but Elena told me that she had not married until she was thirty-six and, in fact, had borne a child out of wedlock when she was in her twenties. The child, a son, had died while still an infant. In the time I knew her, she drank until she began to giggle almost every day.

Carl, Elena's father, had been a detective in the southwestern part of the United States before becoming an attorney. He often said he gained his law degree through a correspondence course, but as he had a reputation for lying—for "bullshitting," as the American expression has it—he may have been lying about this also. I remain convinced that he had been a detective on the North American railroads, however, because he told a number of stories many times and the details never varied. Later in my life, when I had occasion to observe the interrogations of prisoners of war, I found that a clue to the veracity of the prisoner's story could be found in such trivia as whether a farmer wore a brown or a black shirt in every iteration.

Carl was a detective on the railroads during and shortly after the last world war. While many of the stories of his adventures were amusing, all were filled with violence and, often, death. More than once I heard his tale of a shoot-out in a mail car in which he shot one of the thieves two, three, four times, knocking him down every time, but each time the man got up and resumed the gunfight. Only when he ran out of ammunition and was captured did Carl and his partner discover that he had a wooden leg and it was in this leg that Carl had shot him so many times.

Even this story contained an element of sadness, for invariably the thought of his partner recalled the memory of his death, the details of which Carl never confided, at least not in my company. "Damn his eyes," Carl would say, remembering. I do not think I ever knew another man as sad as Carl.

There were other stories. In one he inexplicably turned to his right instead of his left as he stepped away from a boxcar—his habit at this point in his patrol was to turn left—and a brake shoe came down off the roof of the boxcar onto the ground where he would have been walking had he not altered his route an instant before. He had had no idea that a man was lying in wait to murder him.

Another story had him drawing his revolver as he approached a parked automobile, only to find that the man at the steering wheel had a short-barreled shotgun trained on him from behind the door. They stared at each other through the car window until the other man, saying "Just a minute," placed the shotgun on the floor. Carl could not have said what made him take his revolver out of its holster. He had felt the hair on the back of his neck stiffen, so had drawn his gun.

I understood these stories. Only a few months earlier I had foreseen something terrible, yet unknown, happening to me on a parachute jump. That premonition had shown me that the paths our lives take are not made by us, but exist to be discovered. I understood Carl's stories as issuing from a man who had accepted loss and the grief that ensues from it, and who had submitted to forces more powerful than himself and entirely incomprehensible to him. I understood also that this man had raped his daughter and used her for ten years or more, as another man might use a concubine.

Carl was employed by one of the large banks that dealt in Latin American currencies. Exactly what his work consisted of he did not say and I did not ask, as I assumed that anything that concerned banking and currency exchange must be boring. Now, however, I have come to think that Carl was not a banker at all, but used the bank to conceal his real activities, which I believe to have been police work, part of what the North Americans then called "internal defense." I have come to believe this only because it fits with the thrust of his career up until the time he came to Panama.

He had spent his life as a policemen—as a state patrolman in one of the middle western states, as a detective in a city in one of the southern states, as a federal marshal on the railroads and then in the southwestern United States, and finally as operator of his own security agency which he sold in order to come to Panama. He had come south because he had fallen in love with Flora, Elena's mother, while on a vacation cruise through the Western Atlantic, or so he said.

He had always wanted to marry a Latin American woman, he said, and since Flora agreed to have him, he was able to fulfill this fantasy. I used to wonder how someone with such strong racial prejudices could marry, and apparently love, a woman whose skin was so much darker than his own and father a child with her. But eventually, having met in a number of places in the world people who had put aside their color biases in favor of, if not always love, at least marriage, I came to accept this apparent contradiction in some people as irresolvable. Some commentators, of course, do not see it as irresolvable, but it has been a long time since I found materialist explanations satisfactory.

Carl may have taken a law degree at some time, but it was as a policeman that he made his mark. To go from police work of the most adventurous kind to corporate banking does not seem to me to be a likely move. But there was plenty in Central and South America in the time I was there, and after, to occupy a policeman's life. He may have been at least partially responsible for the "disappearances" that struck Latin America like a plague a few years after I left. I admit that I have no evidence for this, only the knowledge that he had been a policeman and was in Central America during one of its most desperate periods, and had the type of personality that could accommodate brutalizing his daughter while remaining so detached from his own barbarities that he could accuse the Latinos of similar crimes with all the righteousness of a Christian zealot. I admit, too, that my loathing for him may have distorted what might otherwise have been a more charitable view of him, and has led me in the direction of speculation rather than fact.

Thirty years after I last saw Carl, I asked a diplomat who

represented Vietnamese interests in Central America to try to ascertain what had become of him, and of Elena. The diplomat could find no evidence of their ever having resided in Panama, although people bearing Elena's mother's clan name could be found in some of the Kuna-inhabited regions of the isthmus.

At last my cast was removed. My leg muscles had atrophied and the leg had sprouted hair where it had not had any before, but I could walk well enough. To celebrate the cast's removal and our engagement, Elena and I decided to go to Panama City. We got on the train in Colón and traveled the length of the canal on it. There were several young soldiers in the same car and I heard one of them refer to the train as "a Jesse James train."

"It's so old, that's why they're calling it that," Elena said. "Jesse James was a train robber in the United States back about a hundred years ago. Some people think he was a hero. My father does."

"Your father? But he was a railroad detective. He would have shot Jesse James if he had caught him on one of his trains."

"I know. It's strange, isn't it?"

We took a room in a modest but comfortable hotel. We unpacked and then Elena went into the bathroom. When she reappeared she was wearing a diaphanous white chemise and panty briefs made of the same material. She seemed shy, even embarrassed. I could not understand this. She who had taken money from me, and presumably from others, for the use of her body—why would she now pretend to be virginal?

Perhaps she wanted to be a virgin again, at least for this moment, so was playing the virgin's part. Yet her shyness seemed genuine. I did not understand her emotions that night.

I have often thought about her and how she looked and what she did and said in that hotel room. I remember that I felt very sad for her, and when I embraced her the first time it was to comfort her, but she interpreted my touch as coming from a different impulse and, in order not to disappoint her, I proceeded, somewhat clumsily, and even reluctantly, to make love to her. And so each of us acted a role, she the shy virgin and I the brute at the mercy of his lust.

After we made love, she said she did not want to make love with me again until after our marriage ceremony. She was serious. I pulled away from her, shaking my head.

"No? Then pay me."

I stared at her.

"You think you can ask me to marry you and then get free pussy?" She laughed. "Come on. Pay up. Forty bucks and I'll do whatever you want, as many times as you want. Come on. It'll be exciting."

I took forty dollars out of my wallet and handed her the bills. She put them on the lamp table beside the bed.

"Come here," she said. "I know what you like."

We spent the next several days doing the things tourists do. We toured the ruins of stone forts and churches, and listened to the guide's talk of pirates and loot and the rape of nuns. We went to the zoo. We went to a sex show and afterward, though Elena seemed genuinely upset by what we had seen, we made love like beasts.

I enjoyed her body immensely and could not get enough of it. I wallowed in her flesh, her heat, the variety of tastes and fragrances that emanated from the different parts of her. Yet even as I used her, I hungered for her, as though the sating of the moment's appetite created an even stronger, more enduring emptiness inside of me that had the quality of the hunger for sustenance. But it had another quality too, a metaphysical one, perhaps, that was even more terrible than the first, one that implanted in my mind as I plunged again and again into Elena's body the vision of an expanding vista of absolute nothingness. I had never known anything like this. I rooted inside her until my penis was too bruised to continue and the skin of her labia was scraped raw so that she winced each time I entered her, holding her grimace until her pleasure had advanced enough that she could give herself up to it. I was trying to deny the emptiness, the void that threatened more and more to overwhelm me with each successive act of coitus. But my method of denial was to copulate again, and this resulted in my confronting the darkness yet another time.

And Elena? What did she want from our congress? If I did not mount her, she mounted me. To see her face in ecstasy was to see a being in flight. I could understand what she would flee from, but she seemed to be reaching *for* something.

After five days we returned to Fort Gulick. We had decided to live together in my room in the BOQ while we looked for an apartment in the city. Of the few officers who lived in the BOQ, a number of them had women stay overnight, or even longer on occasion, so it was unlikely that anyone would complain about Elena's residence there. I had no idea how long it would take to locate an apartment that we could afford. But, if we were going to live together, our only other option was to reside with Elena's parents, and neither she nor I could bear to entertain the thought of that for even a second.

However, in my mail when we returned from Panama City were an acceptance letter from the University of Montana and another from the University of Indiana. It was the University of Montana I elected to attend, for perhaps romantic reasons: I was curious about North American aboriginals who, I had been told, lived in Montana but not in Indiana, despite that state's name.

I had less than three months before classes began. Elena would come with me. We would marry before leaving for Missoula. I would inform my government that I intended to go to graduate school in the United States, using the stipend it had offered.

It was only as I made that decision that I realized my association with the American army was at an end. And suddenly I realized, too, that I hated this army as much as I loved it. I loved it because I loved its soldiers, their dedication and their willingness to embrace hardship and even death in the course of enacting the role their country had written for them. I loved it because of the loyalty, as misshapen as it was sometimes, they had for one another, and because they had accepted me as one of them when their officers rejected me. I hated it for that very rejection that was evident in the contempt I was shown by so many officers, and even some of the more senior NCOs. It is, perhaps, not in keeping with the prestige I have since acquired to dwell on these old emotions, or even to bring them up, but at the present stage of my life, I have no interest in portraying myself as someone born with the solemnity with which I am often depicted by the public media. (For the same reason, I might add, while I recognize the sexual modesty of my own people, if not Americans who may read this book, I have allowed myself to indulge in some explicitness. But the reader will by now be aware of that.)

The next five weeks were taken up by the administrative demands of obtaining my release from the American army and my own, applying for a student visa so I could go to the United States, and arranging transportation to Montana for Elena and myself and some household furnishings Elena had had since childhood. Although I would be Elena's husband, and entitled to reside in the United States, I was not her husband yet, and as I did not know when exactly I would be released from military service, I thought the safest thing would be to apply for a student visa in order to avoid being deported, should my release come before we married.

During those weeks we continued to live in a single room in the BOQ. Constantly in each other's path owing to the smallness of the quarters, we were frequently irritated with each other. While Elena's irritation was broken by the almost daily appearance of Maria, with whom she gossiped about her parents and her friends, mine lay in my stomach like something I shouldn't have eaten. Perhaps also because the room was the scene, or a scene, of Elena's prostitution and of my loneliness, it was an unhappy accommodation for us. I thought often that I had made a mistake in proposing marriage to her, and I wondered if she did not regret accepting my proposal.

Then two things happened to change everything. The

first was an admission. One evening after we returned from supper at the Officers Club I asked, "Where do you go on Tuesday afternoons?" On Tuesdays she would leave post after lunch and return in the evening, sometimes early enough to eat dinner with me at the club, sometimes not. There was always a reason—visiting family friends who had just flown down from the States, going to Panama City to shop with her mother, packing some of her belongings—but her absences were always on Tuesdays.

I asked because that night at the club a young captain had bought her a drink when I was in the restroom. When I returned he was sitting beside her at our table, his arm resting on the back of her chair as they talked. He was not at all embarrassed when I sat down opposite them, but introduced himself and extended his hand to shake mine. From the flush on his cheeks, I gathered that he had had a number of drinks before starting on the one on the table beside his elbow.

Elena was enjoying the attention, and the thought occurred to me that he had been one of her patrons. Certainly he was talking to her as if they already knew each other. Finally she said she had to leave. He leaned over and said something in her ear and she giggled but shook her head no.

Back at the BOQ, she admitted that he had asked her to sleep with him, had, in fact, asked while I was away from the table. She said she could not hear what he whispered to her as we were leaving, but disagreed just to be rid of him.

"Are you going to sleep with him?"

"No! I wouldn't do that to you!"

"Where do you go on Tuesday afternoons?"

"To my father's..." She stopped, and looked up at me—

she had been flipping the pages of a magazine. The expression on her face was one of amazement, I think, at herself for having told me. "...office," she said, completing the sentence. Then she said, "Oh, God."

When I remained silent, she said, "I'm sorry." Tears had already begun to inch down her face.

That night we lay beside each other, trying to sleep. She may not have slept at all. Every time I woke up, she was awake, though silent and still.

In the morning I went to the snack bar alone to drink a cup of coffee, then went to Post Headquarters. I had a number of things to do, but could not concentrate long enough on any of them to accomplish anything. I did not even feel jealous or dishonored. Now, thinking back, I recognize that I was numb from shock, but at the time, I did not know what I felt.

At noon I went back to the BOQ to change into civilian clothes. Elena was not there, but her clothes and jewelry and make-up were. I caught a bus into the city. I looked for a woman I knew but could not find her. I had a drink in a bar and went upstairs with a woman who invited me. Even with her help, I was unable to climax.

When I returned to the BOQ I picked up my mail before going to my room. There was a letter from my mother. Receiving this letter was the second thing that happened that, combined with Elena's admission the night before, altered the direction of my life. I did not immediately open it, but stuffed it in my back pocket and walked to my room. I believed I knew what was in the letter, or at least the effect it would have on me.

Elena was sitting in the chair beside the bed, watching

television—an episode from a western series that I sometimes watched with her.

"I didn't know if you were going to come back," she said.

"Where would I go?"

"I didn't know. Maybe stay with a friend."

"I have no friends."

"I didn't think you were coming back, so I called somebody to come get me. I can call him back if you want."

"Who did you call?"

"My father."

"Ah."

Even as I made that sound, I was not sure what it meant.
Was it pain escaping through my mouth, or was I telling
Elena that I should have guessed as much? Could I have
been that cruel? Even now, I do not know.

She returned her attention to the television. Only then
did I see the two suitcases on the floor beside it.

I left the room to read my mother's letter. In the hallway,
I opened the envelope with my thumbnail, then walked to
the day room and sat in one of the stuffed leather chairs such
as Elena's parents had in their house to read it. My uncle,
my mother's remaining brother, had been arrested. She did
not know where he was; when she went to the city prison,
looking for him, an officer said he had been transferred, but
would not tell her where. His employees did not know what
to do. Unpaid, they were beginning to leave. Even my sister was looking for another job, and had applied for work
with both the Vietnamese and the American armies. I was
the only male left in our family. If I would come home, my
mother wrote, my sister and I could run my uncle's company
until he returned, if he did return. If he did not, the family,

including my uncle's wife and daughters, agreed that my sister and I would take ownership. The country was stable now. While jeeps filled with soldiers and police still patrolled the streets of Saigon, there had been little violence in the city for several weeks.

I replaced the letter in my pocket and walked back to my room. Elena was gone, as were her suitcases.

XI

We do not order our lives as though they are something we can purchase from an American department store catalogue. The roads we travel are not ours to build; it is up to us to discover them, as I had already learned.

I was not meant to be a businessman. I was not drawn to accumulating wealth only in order to accumulate more. My sister saw increasing our wealth as a way to ensure our family's happiness and security. While I did not disagree, I found myself bored by the routine of running a business and gradually left more and more of its operation to her. Finally I left it entirely. We did not see our uncle again until he was released from prison at the end of the war, which was well upon us by the time I was free of my obligations to our company.

On my return to Viet Nam, I had found that nothing was as I expected; everything was more complicated. A number of nationalist and pseudo-nationalist factions claimed the loyalty of those they thought might advance their cause. Some arose from religious sects and secret societies, while others came together out of popular anger, but, in one way or another, all promised rewards if you allied with them and violence if you did not.

I was able to locate my mentor through his sister who still lived in the house where I once had lunch with her and her brother, a house off a main street where Americans could be seen almost daily in expanding numbers and, by early afternoon, diesel fumes overwhelmed the smells from the flowers in the sidewalk stalls and the aromas coming from the cooking grills. Already black market goods were being sold by sidewalk vendors: camouflage uniforms and jungle boots that American soldiers had not even been issued yet, survival knives, cameras, watches, handheld radios—it was clear that the American supply system had established an unintended tributary.

My mentor was a man of even greater depth than I had remembered. Under constant surveillance by the regime now occupying the presidential palace, he nevertheless proved to be an able guide on those roads I found myself traveling. He did not survive the war. Even now, when I am at a loss for insight, I imagine him alive and discuss with him the possible solutions to the difficulty perplexing me. His advice has always enabled me to see aspects of a problem that I would not have seen without it.

Sometimes, even now, when I think about Sergeant Donaldson and Sergeant Hibbard and Corporal Cobb and the other American soldiers I had grown to respect, the knowledge that I betrayed them—not their ideals or their cause (Heaven keep me from acting in any way from ideals or in another's cause), but their assumption that I would remain one with them—strikes me like a blow to the stomach. The possibility that I sponsored an action that resulted in the loss of life of one of them is something I don't dwell on. I used to think that we went to war because we had no choice: diplomacy had failed. I think now that war, the idea of it, is no more than a justification for killing. At its least cynical, it is a justification for killing. At its most intimate, it is killing itself and all that follows from killing.

Sergeant Donaldson told me once that his grandfather was born in Kiev and immigrated to the United States when he was a young man. When America entered World War I, he was told by the War Department that if he volunteered to go into the army, for there was no conscription, he would be given his citizenship when the war was over. He refused. He did not enlist in the army and he never became an American citizen. When Sergeant Donaldson asked him why he refused, his grandfather said that he had a brother in Russia and he did not want to find himself aiming his rifle at a man who would turn out to be his brother. Although Russia and America were allied, the vicissitudes of war could, in a moment, change everything. Once you are committed to war, his grandfather said, you are in control of nothing, not even your own thoughts.

It is a wonderful story, a cautionary tale. And, who knows, it may even be true. If Sergeant Donaldson and I could talk now, I would remind him of what his grandfather told him and ask him what his own thoughts about it were now.

I joined the National Liberation Front because I was tired of the life of a dilettante and I thought that all of the other factions were not serious about anything but their own individual fortunes. I thought this was true of the officer corps of the Army of the Republic, as it called itself, no less than it was of any other faction, although now that I have met and talked with a number of former officers who fought on the side of the South, I must admit that I was in large part wrong.

But I made my choice relatively early in the war, and I was bound to it even when, in years to come, I sometimes doubted that we would be victorious. When the People's Army absorbed the fighting wing of the NLF, I allied myself with the northerners, for by then I saw that our only choices were to adapt or to be cast aside. My early association with the Americans was well known, and because of it, I was always under suspicion. But I proved to have a talent for the kind of war we conducted against them, and my training and experience with the Americans stood me in good stead in that regard. I eventually rose to the rank of colonel, which was more than I expected when I first committed myself to war.

I left the People's Army following the veterans' revolt. This was not what we called it; we referred to "criminal elements," but in fact it was a revolt of our war veterans who had come to believe that their ideals had been betrayed by those who had not fought or sacrificed in the war. I was one of the commanders called upon to suppress the revolt. I did what was required, but took no pleasure in fulfilling my duties. In this, I am able to tell myself, at least I was not like the American general, MacArthur, who went further than he needed to suppress the American veterans in order to satisfy his lust for celebrity. But I cannot conceal from myself that at the end of my career as a soldier, as at the beginning, I betrayed the loyalty and friendship of those soldiers who had trusted me.

I was permitted a small but adequate retirement allowance when I left the army, and permitted also to reside where I chose. I returned to Hue, where I had not been in nearly forty years.

And I returned to poetry. I had been half a lifetime away from it. I am dissatisfied with my efforts and have come to think that I am no longer a poet. My images are strained, my voice does not resonate. I was too long away; I cannot make up for the years I lost. Perhaps I was never truly a poet. If I were, I would have found a way to persevere, regardless of the path my life took. Or perhaps the poet's voice was lost when I embraced as necessary the dishonesty and self-deception that came with being a soldier, or at least a commander.

I never married, though I have known a succession of women with whom I established close relationships. Always I selected women who would betray me. When I discovered this trait in myself, I was appalled and vowed to alter my life so that I might find, if not a wife, then at least a companion. But I did not change my life. At a level below conscious thought, I continued to be drawn to women to whom I was not suited. I think now that I got what I truly wanted. By choosing such women for intimacy, I was inevitably driven back to the ranks of those men whose values and opinions I most cherished.

I think sometimes that had I not come to love Elena, I might have remained with the Americans and fought with their army, or fought on the side of their southern allies, instead of foreswearing my regard for these men. But then I remember that by the time I met Elena, the men whose friendship I most valued had already gone away to war.

JEROME GOLD is the author of thirteen books, including *Sergeant Dickinson*, a novel based on his experience in the US Army Special Forces during the Vietnam War, and *Paranoia & Heartbreak: Fifteen Years in a Juvenile Facility*, taken from the journal he kept during his career as a rehabilitation counselor in a prison for children.